MIDWINTER
INTRIGUE

Tracy Grant

Copyright

NYLA Publishing
121 W. 27th Avenue, Suite 1201, NY 10001, New York.
http://www.nyliterary.com

The Malcolm & Mélanie Suzanne Rannoch Mysteries:

VIENNA WALTZ
IMPERIAL SCANDAL
HIS SPANISH BRIDE
THE PARIS AFFAIR
THE PARIS PLOT
THE BERKELEY SQUARE AFFAIR
LONDON INTERLUDE
THE MAYFAIR AFFAIR
INCIDENT IN BERKELEY SQUARE
LONDON GAMBIT
MISSION FOR A QUEEN
GUILDED DECEIT
MIDWINTER INTRIGUE

forthcoming May 2018
THE DUKE'S GAMBIT

Dedication

For Suzanne, Cordelia, and Malcolm, the feline trio

Acknowledgments

As always, huge thanks to my wonderful agent, Nancy Yost, for her support and insights. Thanks to Natanya Wheeler for once again working her magic to create a beautiful cover and for shepherding the book expertly through the publication process, to Sarah Younger for superlative social media support and for helping the book along through production and publication, and to Amy Rosenbaum and the entire team at Nancy Yost Literary Agency for their fabulous work. Malcolm, Mélanie, and I are all very fortunate to have their support.

Thanks to Eve Lynch for the meticulous and thoughtful copyediting, to Raphael Coffey for magical author photos, and to Kate Mullin for her insights into the story as it developed.

I am very fortunate to have a wonderful group of writer friends near and far who make being a writer less solitary. Thanks to Veronica Wolff and Lauren Willig, who both understand the challenges of being a writer and a mom. To Penelope Williamson, for sharing adventures, analyzing plots, and being a wonderful honorary aunt to my daughter. To Jami Alden, Tasha Alexander, Bella Andre, Allison Brennan, Josie Brown, Isobel Carr, Catherine Coulter, Deborah Crombie, Carol Culver/Grace, Catherine Duthie, Alexandra Elliott, J.T. Ellison, Barbara Freethy, C.S. Harris, Candice Hern, Anne Mallory, Monica McCarty, Brenda Novak, Poppy Reiffin, Deanna Raybourn, and Jacqueline Yau.

Thank you to the readers who support Malcolm and Mélanie Suzanne and their friends and provide wonderful insights on my Web site and social media.

Thanks to Gregory Paris and Jim Saliba for creating and updating a fabulous Web site that chronicles Malcolm and Mélanie Suzanne's adventures. To Kate Mullin, Suzi Shoemake, and Betty Strohecker for managing a wonderful Google+ Discussion Group for readers of the series. Thanks to my colleagues at the Merola Opera Program who help me keep my life in balance. Thanks to Peet's Coffee & Tea and Pottery Barn Kids at The Village, Corte Madera, for welcoming me and my daughter Mélanie and giving me some of my best writing time. And thanks to Mélanie herself, for inspiring my writing, being patient with

Mummy's "work time", and offering her own insights at the keyboard. This is her contribution to this story –

Dramatis Personae

Arriving from Italy and Spain

Malcolm Rannoch, former Member of Parliament and British intelligence agent
Mélanie Suzanne Rannoch, his wife, former French intelligence agent
Colin Rannoch, their son
Jessica Rannoch, their daughter

Laura Fitzwalter, Marchioness of Tarrington, Colin and Jessica's former governess
Lady Emily Fitzwalter, her daughter
Raoul O'Roarke, Laura's lover, Mélanie's former spymaster, and Malcolm's father

Lady Cordelia Davenport
Colonel Harry Davenport, her husband, classical scholar and former British intelligence agent
Livia Davenport, their daughter
Drusilla Davenport, their daughter

At Dunmykel

Malcolm Traquair, Duke of Strathdon, Malcolm's grandfather
Gisèle Thirle, Malcolm's sister
Andrew Thirle, her husband
Ian Thirle, their son

Stephen Drummond, tenant farmer and smuggler
Alec, footman

Guests

Lady Frances Davenport, Malcolm and Gisèle's aunt, Strathdon's daughter
Archibald Davenport, her husband, Harry's uncle
Chloe Dacre-Hammond, Frances's daughter

Aline Blackwell, Frances's daughter
Geoffrey Blackwell, her husband
Claudia Blackwell, their daughter

*Prince Talleyrand, retired French statesman
*Dorothée de Talleyrand-Périgord, his nephew's wife

Oliver Lydgate, Malcolm's university friend

Tommy Belmont, Malcolm's former fellow attaché and agent

"The precious jewel of thy home return."
—Shakespeare, *Richard II*, Act I, scene iii

Chapter 1

Off the coast of Scotland
11 December 1818

Malcolm Rannoch drew the collar of his greatcoat up about his throat. "I don't like it," he said, for probably the hundredth time since they'd left the villa in Italy that had been their home in exile for almost four months.

Mélanie Suzanne Rannoch tucked her arm through her husband's as a gust of wind cut across the prow of the boat. A shower of salt spray shot beneath the hood of her cloak. Probably madness to be on deck in the North Sea in December. Save that the fresh air was welcome after days in the small cabins. And there was no risk of being overheard. Even the crew on deck couldn't make out their words over the wind and sea. Besides, when had she and Malcolm ever been immune to madness? "There wasn't any option." Mélanie said. "Your grandfather is ill. You need to see him."

"There were a lot of options." Malcolm's gaze was fixed on the rolling gray-green of the sea. "You and the children could have stayed in Italy."

"We've been over this, Malcolm. We're safer together."

"So I let myself be convinced."

"You know it's true, darling. You'll never convince me the children and I are safer without you."

His gaze swung from the sea to fasten on her face. "Leaving aside a number of factors. Such as the fact that we're returning to a country where you could be arrested for being a former Bonapartist spy."

She met his granite-hard gray gaze without flinching. "We're going to be in the north of Scotland. We'll be gone before Carfax even knows we're there."

"Ha." Malcolm's bitter laugh cut through the roar of the wind. "Carfax knows everything that happens in Britain."

That, Mélanie acknowledged, considering the head of British intelligence and her husband's former spymaster, was a point. She tried a different tack. "Besides, Carfax doesn't want to have me arrested."

"Didn't when we left six months ago. God knows what he wants now."

"Carfax may know the truth about me, but it still isn't public knowledge. Aunt Frances made that clear when she wrote."

"No." Malcolm's gaze moved back to the shifting water. "But we still don't know who knows. And how or when they may act."

Mélanie pressed her face against Malcolm's shoulder. "I want the children to see their great-grandfather. Dunmykel's on the coast. Half the smugglers in the area are friendly with your family. We can be on a boat at a moment's notice."

"Again, so I allowed you to convince me." Malcolm disengaged his arm from her own so he could wrap it round her shoulders. "I've never been so grateful you're such a formidable agent. I have a feeling we're going to need every skill we both possess."

Mélanie leaned against her husband. She and Malcolm had faced any number of dangerous situations. Highwaymen. Thieves. Enemy agents on both sides. But for all the apparent risks of their return to Britain, those risks weren't what worried her. Malcolm's grandfather, the seemingly indomitable Duke of Strathdon, was ill. Ill enough that Malcolm's sister Gisèle had summoned them out of exile. For all his seeming detachment, Malcolm loved his family. He had changed in the six years of their marriage, and particularly in the past year, in ways she wouldn't have thought possible. But he still held his feelings close. Particularly about his family—not her and their children, but his family in Britain, the family from whom he was separated because of her, the family to whom she was still, in many ways, an outsider. She could guess what he must be feeling, but she knew he wouldn't share it with her. And for all the barriers that had come down between them, she was at a loss as to how to comfort him.

Adventure seemed simple compared to the family drama that lay ahead.

Malcolm held the door against the battering of the wind and steadied his wife as she stepped over the threshold. He ducked his head and followed Mélanie into the tiny main cabin. A remarkably domestic scene greeted them. Harry Davenport, one of the most brilliant agents Malcolm had known in the course of the Peninsular War, was playing a modified version of chess against his own daughter Livia, Malcolm and Mélanie's son Colin, and their friend Emily. Harry's wife Cordelia, once the scandal of the beau monde, was on the opposite bench, reading a story to her toddler Drusilla, and Malcolm and Mélanie's almost-two-year-old Jessica. Laura Tarrington, Emily's mother, who had once been governess to the Rannoch children and was now part of the family, was mending a rent in a small white dress by the swaying light of the oil lamp. Berowne, the cat, was curled up beside her on the bench, batting at the thread.

Malcolm shrugged out of his greatcoat, trying not to spatter water on the floorboards. "We should make land tonight."

Colin looked up, a rook in one hand. "And we'll be able to see Great-Grandpapa?"

"In the morning, if not tonight. He may need to rest. Though knowing my grandfather, ten to one he'll be up and about by the time we get there."

Colin's gaze told Malcolm his son saw this for the fiction it was, but, at the advanced age of five and a half, he wasn't going to say so in front of the younger children. Malcolm smiled at his son.

"I like Dunmykel," Livia said.

"The weather will be a lot different from when you saw it in the summer, sweetheart," Harry told his daughter.

"I know," Livia said. "I like snow."

Drusilla bounced on the opposite seat. "Christmas!"

Malcolm looked at Mélanie and then at Harry, as a crossfire of glances shot between the adults. Two more days until Jessica's birthday on 13 December. Two more weeks until Christmas. And while holidays might seem of little moment to the adults with everything else that was going on, they were as important as ever to the children.

"And we'll have Christmas in Scotland in the snow," Cordelia said. "What could be more agreeable? A roaring fire in that marvelous fireplace and garlands on the stair rail."

"And mistletoe," Livia said. "You can kiss Daddy."

"Quite right," Cordelia said. "Not that I need an excuse."

"Hot chocolate," Colin said.

"Mulled wine," Harry murmured.

"Do you have oranges?" Emily asked. "We used to at the school."

Emily had spent her first four years at an orphanage, lost to her mother. This would be her first Christmas with her mother and the Rannochs.

Laura smiled at her daughter, though Malcolm caught the brightness in her eyes. "Always, darling. Lots and lots of them."

"Presents," Jessica said.

"Lots and lots of presents," Malcolm said with a smile.

The boat swayed. Mélanie, who had gone to scoop up Berowne, turned and met Malcolm's gaze, the cat draped over her shoulder, her blue-green eyes dark as a midnight sea. Malcolm knew the trunks they had brought with them were more than half-filled with presents. They had that part taken care of. But somehow, whatever faced them at Dunmykel, they were going to have to capture holiday magic for the children.

Dunmykel surged on a cliff above the bay, its walls, a brilliant white by day, now a dark outline against a darker sky, illumined by an almost full moon that had broken through the clouds as they pulled up to the dock. Torches burned on either side of the wrought-metal gate that led to his mother's gardens, their light sparking off the gilding. The air smelled of salt and cold and home.

Malcolm drew a deep breath. His senses quickened and something tugged in his chest that might have been recognition, or relief. Or fear. This was hardly the way he'd been accustomed to arrive at Dunmykel. But as boys, he and his friend Andrew Thirle (now his brother-in-law) had gone out on more than one late-night expedition. And he'd left or returned this way from the occasional mission. Once or twice he'd slipped across the sea accompanied by his mother, on what he now realized were missions of her own.

Mélanie slipped her gloved hand into his own and squeezed his fingers. She was holding Jessica. Colin, Emily, and Livia were at the rail, heedless of the cold, eyes fixed on the sight before them.

"It's a castle." Emily's voice carried on the wind.

"There's a sliding panel," Colin said. "And a secret passage down to the beach."

"But we'll go in the conventional way, at least this first time," Malcolm said.

Laura, Harry, and Cordy, with Drusilla in her arms, joined them.

MIDWINTER INTRIGUE

"Down." Drusilla wriggled against Cordelia's hold.

"Wait until we dock, darling. The deck's slippery."

And the wind strong enough to topple a toddler. Malcolm was keeping a sharp eye on the older three at the rail.

"Here." Harry took Drusilla from his wife and swung her up on his shoulders, hands firmly grasping her booted ankles. "You can see better this way."

Drusilla gave a crow of delight. She was fearless, like her father. Malcolm half expected Jessica to demand the same, but she was clinging to Mélanie, fingers tight on her mother's cloak, head pressed to Mélanie's shoulder, as though on some level she grasped the implications of their arrival.

Two of the crew lashed ropes round the pilings as they pulled up to the dock, then handed the passengers from the swaying boat. In the moonlight, Malcolm saw three figures hurrying along the steep steps down the cliffside from the house. He and Harry lifted the older children onto the dock and debarked last, Malcolm carrying Berowne's covered basket. By that time, the three figures were on the gravel path approaching the gates. The torchlight caught the bright hair of a woman who was in the lead.

"Malcolm!" His sister Gisèle pushed open the gate and ran forwards to fling her arms round him.

Malcolm hugged his sister tightly. The top of her head still barely reached his shoulder, but she was twenty, almost two years married, and the mother of a nine-month-old. He'd seen her in Italy only two months ago, but being countries apart made the separation seem greater.

"The boat signaled us. We've been watching for days." Gisèle drew back to look up at him. Her blue eyes, so like their mother's, held both relief and worry. And something else, as though she wasn't sure quite how much she should say. "Oh, I'm so glad you're here. All of you."

Gisèle ran to hug Mélanie and the children. Malcolm set down Berowne's basket and went to embrace his boyhood friend Andrew, now Gisèle's husband. That was when he recognized the second man, standing a bit in the shadows. Good God.

"O'Roarke." Malcolm said. "Why am I not surprised?"

Since childhood, Malcolm had been used to Raoul O'Roarke's unexpected appearances and disappearances. That was even more the case in recent years, when he had learned that O'Roarke was his biological father and also that he had been a French spy and Mélanie's spymaster. A tangle of revelations from which they had somehow emerged a fragile family.

Malcolm moved to hug his father. Raoul's arms closed quick and hard round him. His fingers pressed against the back of Malcolm's head for a moment, in a way that brought a shock of memory from childhood. But before either could speak, a cry cut the air.

"Daddy!" Emily ran to throw her arms round Raoul's legs. O'Roarke might not be her biological father, but he was certainly her parent now. He scooped her up as Colin ran to join them, and Jessica and Drusilla wriggled to be put down. One of the most formidable spymasters in the Peninsular War dropped to his knees on the dock, enveloped in a cluster of small children. When he stood up, he somehow had Jessica on his shoulders, Drusilla in one arm, and Emily holding his other hand. They met the other adults in the middle of the dock.

With his arms still full of children, Raoul leaned in to kiss Laura, making no pretense that their relationship was anything other than it was. "You look well."

"So do you," Laura said, relief evident in her voice.

"She doesn't get sick to her stomach anymore," Emily said.

"I'm relieved to hear it," Raoul said. Though his eyes held the wonder and terror of an incipient father. And the guilt of a man who has been too long away from the mother of his child.

Malcolm studied his father. "Our letter got to you quickly. Or did Gelly write to you as well?" *And is Grandfather really that ill?* was the subtext, though Malcolm wouldn't say so in front of the children.

"Gisèle wrote to me." Raoul's voice was level, his gaze warm and steady on Malcolm's own.

Which meant the situation was even more serious than Malcolm had believed.

"Great-Grandpapa's sick." Colin rarely missed anything in adult interactions.

"I know." Raoul smiled at him. "Your Great-Grandpapa's always had a remarkable constitution, so I daresay we're all fussing about nothing, but it's too long since we've all seen him. And each other."

"He'll be glad you're here. All of you." Gisèle hugged her arms over her chest.

Andrew shot a quick look at her but merely went to give the sailors directions about the luggage. Two footmen who had followed

6

MIDWINTER INTRIGUE

Andrew, Gisèle, and Raoul from the house came forwards now the family greetings were over.

"Do come in out of the cold," Gisèle said. "We have refreshments in the house."

They went through the metal gates into a world at once familiar and alien. It was more than a year since Malcolm had seen his mother's gardens, and they were mostly dormant in December. But he could name each flower bed by memory, trace a path through the hedged walkways even in the shadows, pick out the griffin and dragon from the Rannoch arms in the knotted parterre, see the shadowy outline of the sundial and the reflecting pool surrounded by roses pruned back for winter. The steps were the same, the worn granite he'd run up and down so often as a boy. That he'd slipped down at night to warn the locals who were smuggling. Lanterns lit their way from the terrace and candles burned in the drawing room beyond the French windows. But Gisèle led the way through this room and down the passage beyond to the breakfast parlor. Though it was dark out, pots of tea and coffee steamed on the table, a bottle of wine was open on the sideboard, and plates of bannocks, cheese, fruit, and nuts filled the table. Malcolm met his sister's gaze. Funny how the smell of bannocks brought back childhood. "You're an angel, Gelly."

Gisèle smiled, "We weren't sure when you'd get here, but we thought you'd be hungry. It's all cold but there's plenty of it."

The children fell on the food with enthusiasm. Malcolm sipped a cup of coffee and buttered a bannock but didn't take more than a few bites. After a short time, Gisèle excused herself. The children peppered Raoul with questions about when he'd left Spain, and what his journey had been like, and asked Andrew about baby Ian and when they could see the sliding panel, in between recounting highlights of their own journey. Easy enough to sip coffee and nod while the childish voices covered any awkwardness. He hadn't missed the measured look Gisèle and Andrew had exchanged before she left the room.

Gisèle slipped back into the room, stood listening to the children with a smile for a moment, then said, "Grandfather's awake. He's not up to a lot of visitors, but he'd like to see you, Malcolm—"

"Of course." Malcolm pushed his chair back.

"And Mélanie. And Raoul."

Mélanie put Jessica in Cordelia's arms and got to her feet, but Raoul stared at Gisèle. "My dear Gisèle, I hardly think—"

7

"Please, Raoul." Gisèle's voice held an edge of desperation. "He was quite definite. And I don't want to do anything to upset him just now."

Raoul cast a quick look at Laura, then nodded and got to his feet while Andrew promised the children some cakes to make up for their having to wait to see the duke. In truth, smiling at the children, Malcolm thought their feelings were mixed. Illness could be frightening to confront.

"How about some more milk?" Harry said. "And I think we have enough salt and pepper pots for a siege."

Gisèle conducted Malcolm, Mélanie, and Raoul up the main stairs to the suite of rooms the Duke of Strathdon had occupied on visits to Dunmykel for as long as Malcolm could remember. For all Strathdon was a reclusive scholar, he'd always been tough, Malcolm reminded himself. Difficult to imagine the world without his acerbic presence.

Mélanie reached for his hand again and squeezed his fingers. Malcolm cast a quick smile at her, warmed by what he saw in her eyes, and drew a breath to confront whatever faced them in his grandfather's room.

Chapter 2

Gisèle threw open the door. The familiar smell of Strathdon's shaving soap washed over Malcolm, mixed with the aromas of whisky and lavender. Light glowed from an Argand lamp and two braces of candles. Malcolm's gaze went first to the bed, a carved-oak Elizabethan four-poster hung with red velvet. The coverlet was smooth, the pillows undisturbed. It was a moment before Malcolm saw the figure standing by the windows, outlined by the cloud-filtered moonlight. And another moment before he realized it was his grandfather.

Strathdon was wrapped in a blue brocade dressing gown, but when he turned the light caught the gleam of a pristine white shirt and an immaculately tied cravat beneath. And glittered off the crystal of the glass he held, half full of whisky.

Malcolm stepped further into the room and surveyed his grandfather, suspicion beginning to take hold in his mind. He fixed the duke with a level gaze. "Sir? You look well."

Strathdon's eyes glinted blue in the shadows. "You sound relieved. And a bit suspicious."

"Damnably acute as always, sir. On both counts."

Strathdon gave a grunt of acknowledgment that was half a laugh. "Suzanne, my dear. Or I suppose I must get used to calling you Mélanie now."

Malcolm felt his wife's sudden stillness, though she spoke with scarcely a pause and in a voice that would sound tranquil to almost any ears but his own. "Yes, I've gone back to using it. It's what my parents called me. I couldn't bear it for a time after they died, but now I find it comforting. I suppose Gisèle told you when she came back from Italy."

"So she did." Strathdon smiled. It was an unusually expansive smile for his grandfather, and somehow not reassuring in the least. "O'Roarke. Thank you for breaking away from your revolutions. I'm flattered."

"You must know the pull this family have always had on me, sir," Raoul said. His voice too was easy, though Malcolm caught the undertones, a mix of steel and frayed rope.

"Sit down." Strathdon waved a hand towards the settee and chairs before the fireplace with a courtesy that was almost a command. "Perhaps you'd pour some whisky for everyone, Malcolm. Gisèle, you can go back to the other guests and reassure them I'm not at death's door."

Gisèle met their grandfather's gaze for a moment, cast a glance at Malcolm that might have held apology, and gave a quick nod.

"Don't blame, Gisèle," Strathdon added when she had left the room. "She's a spirited young woman, but I was most insistent."

Malcolm filled glasses with his grandfather's favorite whisky and passed them round. He took a strong swallow himself before dropping down on the settee beside Mélanie.

Strathdon settled back in one of the chairs and took an appreciative, though less large, sip from his own glass. He looked for all the world as though he were enjoying himself. He'd always been pale, but the candlelight showed a healthy glow to his skin. His gaze was razor sharp as it shot from Malcolm to Mélanie to Raoul. "You can't imagine," he said, in a pleasant and quite implacable voice, "that I would read the letter you were so obliging as to send me and not question why my grandson and his wife and children were departing abruptly for Italy with no apparent plans to return."

Malcolm curled his fingers round the arm of the settee. "I told you—"

"You were tired and needed time away. You're never tired, Malcolm. Let's not waste time pretending I don't know things. I know Carfax drove you abroad. I know what secrets he threatened to expose. My daughter and my new son-in-law have been back in Britain for some time, you know."

Malcolm drew in a breath. His aunt Frances had married Archibald Davenport, Harry's uncle and a colleague of Raoul's, in Italy in the early autumn. "I should have—"

"Yes?" Strathdon settled back in his chair and crossed his legs. "In fairness to Fanny and Archie, they only confirmed what I had already learned from another source. I may not be an agent, but the three of you aren't the only ones with sources of information in France, you know."

Malcolm held his grandfather's gaze with his own. "Talleyrand." The wily former French foreign minister knew far too many of their secrets. What Malcolm hadn't considered properly was that Talleyrand had been his grandfather's friend long before he himself was born. "You didn't—"

"Commit anything to writing? Of course not. I met him secretly on the French coast. Quite an adventure. I can't say I'd want to be an agent, but I do understand the allure of the work you all engage in." Strathdon turned his gaze to Mélanie. "I always knew you were brilliant, my dear, but it seems I woefully underestimated you."

Mélanie was sitting absolutely still beside Malcolm, hands gripped round her whisky glass, knuckles white. "You flatter me, Your Grace. Unless you mean you underestimated my duplicity."

Strathdon's gaze moved between Mélanie and Malcolm. "I've seen the two of you together. I may not be the most discerning when it comes to affairs of the heart, but one can't spend as much time as I have studying the works of Shakespeare without acquiring some appreciation of the nuances. And then I had the benefit of Fanny's and Archie's insights." He regarded Mélanie a moment longer. "I understand your parents were actors."

Mélanie swallowed. "Yes."

"And you were an actress yourself."

"For a time, yes." Before her family had been killed, before she'd lived on the streets, before she'd found a bleak refuge in a brothel. Malcolm wondered just how much of his wife's history his grandfather knew. Surely not all. Aunt Frances and Archie and Talleyrand didn't know those details.

Strathdon nodded. "I knew you named your daughter for Shakespeare's Jessica. I didn't realize you played her."

"And Juliet and Perdita. The changeling boy in *Midsummer* when I was a baby. The young Duke of York when I was eight. I always wanted to play Viola. And Beatrice."

Strathdon nodded again, something that might have been approval crossing his face. For the duke, fidelity to Shakespeare was far more important than fidelity to Britain. His gaze moved on to Raoul and settled, cool and neutral.

"I don't really see," Raoul said, "why you should be remotely forbearing when it comes to me."

Strathdon gave a grunt of acknowledgement. "Fanny said she wanted to murder you."

"Fanny would have been entitled to murder me."

11

"She also said by the time she left Italy she'd never loved you more."

"My dear sir. I can't imagine Frances Dacre-Hammond—Frances Davenport—saying anything of the sort."

"Quite unlike her," Strathdon agreed. "I don't remember any of her other pregnancies turning her so emotional. But then I don't remember her ever being so besotted with the father of her child."

"I imagine Fanny would hit you if you called her besotted."

"Probably," Strathdon agreed. He regarded Raoul for another long moment. "I know what you meant to my eldest daughter. And I know what she put you through."

Raoul cleared his throat. "If you know what I meant to Arabella, you know more about her than I was ever able to discover. But she did mean a great deal to me."

"You gave her happy moments," Strathdon said, his voice gruffer than usual. "Thinking back, I'm inestimably grateful for that."

"None of which excuses what I did later," Raoul said.

"You made choices," Strathdon said. "All three of you. You seem to have found a way to live with them. I'm not sure it's for me to judge or interfere. Though I might have been a good deal more angry had I not heard Fanny's view of the situation, I confess."

Raoul drew a breath. "Fanny is inclined to ro—"

"Romanticize things? Now whom do you think she'd be hitting?" Strathdon took a sip of whisky. "What concerns me now is less what caused you all to leave Britain than how to get you back."

Malcolm leaned forwards, fingers clenched round his glass. "Your concern means a great deal, Grandfather. But you're meddling in things you don't understand."

"I understand it's intolerable for my grandson and his wife and children to live in exile."

"You're a powerful man, Grandfather. But you can't always remake the world the way you want it."

"Isn't remaking the world precisely what you all want to do?" Strathdon asked.

"Believe me, we have a better chance of passing electoral reform and Catholic Emancipation and overturning the Spanish monarchy than of making it safe for us to return to Britain."

"For shame, Malcolm. I thought you had more vision. I'm sure you do, O'Roarke. And you, Suzanne. Mélanie."

MIDWINTER INTRIGUE

Malcolm felt his wife's hesitation. He knew, though they seldom spoke of it, that she still harbored hopes they'd be able to return home. That is, to Britain.

"Italy's not so bad," Malcolm said, gaze on his grandfather. "You can visit us whenever you like."

"I don't give a damn where you choose to live. If you choose to live in Italy, I will make no attempt to stop you. I do care very much that you be free to choose to live where you wish. And to do the work that you wish."

"I don't need to be back in Parliament—"

"Darling." Mélanie put a hand on his arm. "I'm not saying we can go back. But don't lie to your grandfather."

Malcolm swung his gaze from her to Strathdon. "We're fine."

"That," said Strathdon, "is not satisfactory. I imagine it's quite a hindrance to O'Roarke's work as well."

"That's hardly a consideration," Raoul said.

"No?" Strathdon lifted a brow. "You've sacrificed enough for it. It was quite important to Arabella as well."

Raoul kept his gaze steady. "I think we all agree we want what's best for Malcolm and Mélanie and the children. Irritating as it is, Carfax is a formidable opponent."

Strathdon turned his glass in his hand. "I always sensed Carfax was ruthless, though obviously you know far more than I do. Believe me, I take the risks to all of you seriously."

"Then, for God's sake—" Malcolm said.

"Which is why I would never have dreamed of luring you back here did I not have a plan to checkmate Carfax."

Malcolm froze, gaze locked on his grandfather. Strathdon wore his ducal mantle relatively lightly compared to some of his contemporaries. But he had a tendency to consider himself omnipotent. "Sir, believe me, I appreciate your efforts. I'm sure we all do. But we can't—"

"I have no illusions I can protect you on my own. But I have friends arriving in a few days who will be able to help."

"Sir—"

"Friends you can trust implicitly. Do me the favor of at least waiting until they arrive, Malcolm. Until you've heard my plan out in full. I assume having come all this way you'll at least stay and keep Christmas at Dunmykel."

Malcolm drew a harsh breath. His wife gripped his arm. "You couldn't send us away," she told the duke.

Strathdon inclined his head. "Thank you, my dear."

Much remained to be said, but it could not be dealt with tonight. They moved to the door. Before he followed Mélanie and Raoul into the passage, Malcolm turned back to Strathdon. "I love you, Grandfather."

Strathdon gave a faint, dry smile. "Thank you, my boy. I trust you know the sentiment is returned."

Malcolm prowled across the bedchamber he and Mélanie shared. "He played us."

"You have to admit it was cleverly done," Raoul said. "I always knew Strathdon noticed far more than he lets on, but I confess he surprised me. In retrospect, I probably should have realized he'd try to bring you back."

Malcolm spun round to face his father. "We can't go back."

"Could you?" Cordelia asked. "I mean, if there's any chance—"

"There isn't," Malcolm said.

His voice, Mélanie thought, was like the flat of a sword. They were all in the bedchamber, she and Malcolm, Raoul and Laura, Harry and Cordy, sharing explanations and a second round of whisky.

"Darling," she said. "I agree it's unlikely. But we underestimated his enterprise in bringing us back. We should at least listen to his plan."

Malcolm raked a hand through his hair. "I have no intention of leaving until after the New Year. Unless something happens. But I have very little faith in a plan he has to wait to even tell us about."

"Perhaps he thinks these friends he's waiting for will be more persuasive," Laura said.

"I strongly suspect the 'friends' are Talleyrand," Raoul said.

"Yes, so do I. Otherwise I'd be more worried." Malcolm prowled across the room again. "Even if the plan is flawless, even if somehow it could believably checkmate Carfax, too many people know. Now Grandfather knows. God knows what Gelly and Andrew have pieced together at this point. They asked so few questions in Italy, I had suspicions about what they guessed even then. And after these machinations—Of course, I trust Gelly and Andrew and Grandfather with my life, but the more people who know—"

"Containing information." Harry swirled the whisky in his glass. "The spy's nightmare. Or one of the spy's nightmares. Every person who has information is a point of vulnerability."

"Why I preferred to run my own networks and coordinate with Paris as little as possible," Raoul said. "Much less risk of exposure. But we're still talking about a finite circle that we know of."

"That we know of," Malcolm said. He scraped a hand over his face, then dropped down on the chintz-covered dressing table bench beside Mélanie. "I'm sorry. I'm usually not such a font of negativity."

"It's easy to be negative when one's afraid to hope," Harry said. "Take it from one who lived his life that way for four years."

Cordelia reached for her husband's hand. "But sometimes one needs hope to take a risk. God knows those risks can be worth it."

"And sometimes one is right to fear the risk." Malcolm took a swallow of whisky. "We'll stay here and enjoy Christmas. I'll listen to what Grandfather has to say. Then we're going back to Italy."

15

Chapter 3

Mélanie went up to her husband and slid her arms round him. "I know it's frustrating. And an adjustment after what we thought we were facing. But it's also a relief."

"That Grandfather isn't really ill?" Malcolm rested his chin on her hair. "Of course it is. And it's good to see him. It's good to—"

She drew her head back to look up at him. "See Dunmykel?"

"I was going to say Gelly and Andrew, but yes, it's good to be back at Dunmykel. I just can't bear to think of the disappointment in Grandfather's eyes when he realizes his plan won't work. I can't bear to think of—"

"Your own disappointment?" Mélanie touched his cheek.

He caught her hand and drew it across his mouth. "I was going to say yours."

"But I'm not the only one afraid to hope."

He laced his fingers through her own. "We're happy in Italy. We're making a life. Would you even want to go back to London?"

"We couldn't." She swallowed and held his gaze. "Not to the life we had before. Not entirely. Not to Almack's and dinners and balls at the heart of the beau monde. And it has nothing to do with Carfax."

Malcolm's gaze flickered across her face. "Laura."

"You know the talk there'll be about the baby. It goes without saying we wouldn't be invited certain places. Places I'd be quite relieved not to return to, for the most part. I just want to make sure the thought of it doesn't make Laura do anything silly."

A shadow of concern crossed Malcolm's face, but he said, "Laura's a sensible woman. She knows we're highly unlikely to be able to go back to London, in any case."

"Highly unlikely?"

"You know how I dislike most categorical statements."

"You've been making rather a lot of them tonight."

"I was concerned."

She put her hands on his chest. "We couldn't be at the heart of the beau monde. But you could still be in Parliament. I wouldn't have vouchers to Almack's, but you probably wouldn't be blackballed at Brooks's. I might not be able to be the sort of asset to you as a wife that I once was, but—"

"For God's sake, Mel. Your brilliance and judgment and way with words would always make you an asset. I don't want a career based on having a hostess. One of the things we've gained from all this is to be free of some of our old roles. You can't tell me you wouldn't be happy to be done with it."

"Some of it," she said with honesty. "Though I'm surprised at how much I'd miss. But it's good to know we could go on in Britain without that side of things."

"Sweetheart." He touched his fingers to her cheek as though she were something fragile. Or perhaps as though what was between them was something fragile. "You can't—"

"Get my hopes up? I'm not. I'm just considering eventualities. We've both always considered every eventuality we could, even remote ones."

"I don't—"

"Malcolm." Mélanie curled her fingers over her husband's own where they rested on her cheek, and asked a question she'd first asked in Italy. "What do you want?"

"I want you to know I'll be happy going back to Italy. That in many ways going back will be a relief."

"Well, then." She reached up to kiss him. "We have nothing to worry about."

But she hadn't missed the longing in his eyes at the sight of the Scottish coast. Or when they talked about Parliament. She knew full well what they'd found in each other. But she also knew what Malcolm had given up because of her.

"Thoughtful of Gisèle to put us in the same room." Laura's voice sounded slightly husky to her own ears, as she stepped into their room, in the fifteenth-century part of the house, with mullioned windows and a bed of mellowed oak that looked to be over a hundred years old, hung with flowered cream curtains that battled the chill. "Of course, she saw how we were living in Italy."

Raoul pushed the door of the bedchamber to behind them. "I find myself grateful to the Duke of Strathdon for reasons that have nothing to do with this plan of his."

"I was thinking much the same." Laura touched her fingers to the gold chain round her neck. Raoul's signet ring was threaded on it, tucked beneath the black velvet that edged the French gray merino of her traveling gown. He almost never spoke of the family he'd grown up in, but he'd worn the signet ring every day for as long as she'd known him. Then, before he left for Spain the last time, he'd pulled the ring from his finger and put it on her own. Without speaking. But then a lot between them had never been defined by words.

She pulled the ring free of her bodice, turned, and stepped into his arms. "Will you be able to stay until Strathdon's plan is sorted out?"

"Oh, yes. I was going to try to get to Italy for Christmas, in any case." His arms closed round her. "Not that Christmas in and of itself means anything particular to me. But sharing it with all of you would. It's bad enough I was gone for Emily's birthday."

Taking advantage of the time they had. It was how they had always made their relationship work. She tilted her head back and pulled his head down for a kiss. Warmth and comfort and longing washed over her. But midway through, she pulled back.

"What is it, sweetheart?" he asked.

She seized his hand and put it on her stomach. "Our son or daughter is active. Wait a moment. Once the kicks start they usually come thick and fast."

He went still, the sort of light in his eyes that they got when he was in search of a clue. His fingers moved over her stomach. She saw the flash in his eyes when the baby kicked again, against the palm of his hand. "You seem to have a mind of your own, little one," he murmured.

"It runs in the family," Laura said.

Raoul looked up and met her gaze, his own suspiciously bright. "You're better, truly?"

"Oh, yes. I never was so very ill. Just the occasional stretch when I couldn't stomach much more than soda water and biscuits. But in the middle months of pregnancy one feels almost indecently well. It was the same with Emily."

He drew a breath and glanced away. "I wish—"

"There'll be time." She put up a hand and turned his face back to her own. "Time for you to fuss over me. Days of waiting at the end where you can do your best to distract me. Time to plan—not that we're ever able to plan very much." She scanned her lover's face. "Do you think there's any chance Strathdon's plan could work?"

He was silent for a fraction of a second. "You heard what I said when we all discussed it."

"I did. I thought you might be tempering your response one way or another so Malcolm and Mélanie aren't disappointed. Or so Malcolm isn't even more inclined to dismiss the idea out of hand."

He gave a faint smile, though his gaze had gone serious. "It's difficult to even hazard a guess when we haven't heard the plan yet. The past has taught me not to underestimate Strathdon. But Malcolm's right, it's not just checkmating Carfax, as Herculean as that task seems. A damnable number of people know the truth. Each one is a risk. And even Mélanie is less inclined to run risks these days."

"Even you are."

"Even I am. More so than I've ever been in my life." He slid his hand behind her neck. "You're on British soil. It would be reasonably safe for you to visit your family."

She nodded. "I've thought about it. Even thought about asking my father and Sarah to meet me partway. Harry said he'd escort Emily and me."

Raoul's brows drew together. "I should go with you. They'll have questions."

"I thought about that too. But I'm not sure how safe it is for you to leave the Highlands. I'll never forgive you if you're arrested before the baby's born."

He drew a breath, then nodded. "I'd like to see them. And explain. At some point I should talk to your parents. But perhaps better for a number of reasons that you see them first. Your parents and your brother-in-law and sister-in-law would rightly wish me at the devil."

"Darling." Laura slid her arms round him. "Both my father and Sarah, and James and Hetty, will be well aware that my pregnancy is at least as much my responsibility as yours. I know you, of all people, wouldn't make the mistake of treating me as though I'm not responsible for my own actions."

He grinned. "Caught." But the concern was still there in his eyes.

"I wrote to my father and Sarah," she said. "They know about the baby. They wished us well."

19

His eyes widened.

"I know," she said. "But my father's always been surprisingly good at seeing past convention, and I think I've underestimated Sarah in that regard. I suspect they both probably saw more than we realized before we left Britain. I haven't written to James and Hetty yet, but I will before they hear about the baby another way. It's a bit harder for them. I don't want them to be touched by scandal." She swallowed. "I don't want Malcolm and Mélanie to be touched by it. If there's any chance they can go back—"

His hands settled on her shoulders. "Laura—"

"We said it when we first talked about the baby. That in Italy the scandal mattered less. That it would be different if we were still in Britain. If there were a chance to go back to their old lives—"

"Laura, no." His grip on her shoulders tightened. "You can't let yourself think that way."

"Tell me you aren't thinking about yourself as a liability to them."

"That's different. I'm—"

"I'm more of a scandal than you are, my darling. Given how the world views women."

"Malcolm and Mélanie would never forgive you for talking about yourself that way, sweetheart. You've always reminded us all of what it means to be a family. You've believed in that when I wasn't brave enough to do so. For God's sake, don't waver now. I need you."

Laura stared up at her lover. The sharp bones of his face. The hooded gray eyes that burned with intelligence. The ironic mouth. When she'd first met him, he'd claimed to be a cold-blooded strategist. "You're diabolical, Raoul O'Roarke."

He raised a brow. "I've been called that before, but not in these circumstances."

"You never admit to needing anything. Or anyone. And then you say it to me just when you need me to do what you want."

"That's not—"

"Don't lie to me, darling. Look me in the eye and tell me you'd have said it for any other reason."

He stared down at her. Oddly, his gaze was more open than usual. "I don't say it easily. And I might not have said it in other circumstances. But that doesn't mean it isn't true." He pressed a kiss to her forehead and held her against him for a moment. "Quite the reverse, in fact." His fingers trembled against her cheek. "I know how to be alone.

MIDWINTER INTRIGUE

It isn't the most comfortable existence, but it's relatively simple. I've had a disastrous marriage, and a son I tried to raise without being able to acknowledge him. I don't really have a clue about having a family."

"Nor do I, if it comes to that. We're rather working it out together."

"I'd say you have more of a knack for it than I do."

She shook her head. "My marriage makes yours look like a success. I've had Emily with me for less than a year. But I spent enough time alone to know how cold a life it is. It's worth holding on to what we have."

"My point precisely." He pulled her closer but looked down at her instead of kissing her. "It's easier being alone, in a lot of ways. But God help me, I wouldn't go back. I never stop thinking how fortunate I am."

Laura tangled her fingers in his hair and pulled his head down for a kiss. "There's something else about the middle months of pregnancy. One has the most indecent longing for one's child's father in all sorts of ways."

Mélanie smoothed the covers over Jessica in her cradle. She'd woken, fretful, her nappy wet, but had been back asleep before Mélanie was even finished changing her. Mélanie glanced towards the walnut four-poster. Malcolm, uncharacteristically, hadn't woken. His even breathing told her that he slept still. A sign of how exhausted he was. Not that she needed a sign. He'd scarcely slept on the journey from Italy. But she was relieved he was actually able to sleep now. Perhaps on some level he knew they had a brief respite before they were going to need their wits about them again.

Berowne was curled up at the foot of the bed, one paw draped over Malcolm's feet. Their trunks were piled against the wall, including the two carefully packed with presents for Jessica's birthday the day after tomorrow, and then for Christmas. Blanca, Mélanie's maid and companion, and Blanca's husband Miles Addison, Malcolm's valet, had remained in Italy with their infant son and Addison's parents who were visiting. But Mélanie was used to turning temporary lodgings into a home. Time enough tomorrow to unpack, make these rooms their own, make sure she had everything organized for her daughter's second birthday. Time to examine whatever plan Strathdon offered and see if there was any chance it could work. One moment at a time. That was how she'd got through the past six months. That was how she'd got through the past ten years.

She touched her fingers to Jessica's head, then started back towards the bed, but midway across the room a sound stopped her. A faint stir or creak from the adjoining room that had become the night nursery, as it was in Italy, as it had been in Berkeley Square (rather than the rooms deep in the north wing that had been the nursery in Malcolm and Gisèle's childhood). She crossed the room and eased open the door. The tin-shaded night light cast a faint glow over the canework beds and flowered quilts. And over the tall, lean figure sitting on the edge of one of the beds.

Raoul looked up and gave a crooked smile. "Emily had a bad dream and half woke. Fortunately, Colin and Livia slept through it. Laura too, remarkably enough."

"Pregnancy is exhausting. Thank goodness she can sleep." Mélanie moved into the room and smoothed the covers over Colin. His hair had fallen over his face the way Malcolm's did sometimes when he slept. She ran her fingers through it, savoring the abandon in the way he was sprawled beneath the covers and the steadiness of his breathing. "Oh, to be able to lose oneself in sleep."

"Thank God they still can." Raoul tucked Emily's stuffed rabbit into the crook of her arm and gave Livia, sleeping beside her, her stuffed cat to hold.

"I'm relieved they aren't having more nightmares." Mélanie patted Colin's stuffed bear.

"You've done a remarkable job of keeping their lives stable."

"We all have." Mélanie sat on the edge of Colin's bed. "Malcolm didn't wake either. He's exhausted. Between being on guard in case we were followed on the journey and worrying what we'd find when we got here, he's scarcely slept since we left Italy. He'll be able to think more clearly when he's had some rest."

Raoul tucked the quilt round Emily and Livia. "He seemed to be thinking quite clearly tonight." He held her gaze in the steady glow of the night light. "I know how much you want to give him back what he's lost, *querida*. Believe me, I do too. But even in my most reckless days I recognized that sometimes risks are too high."

Mélanie looked at her son, the tangle of brown hair against the white pillow, the curve of his lashes against his skin, the soft line of his mouth. He was such a person now, but when he slept, somehow she could see straight back to his babyhood. "I'm trying to be cautious, whatever everyone thinks. But we'll always run risks, wherever we go. If there's a chance we could be here—"

"Impossible to even speculate until we hear Strathdon's plan," Raoul said.

Mélanie spread her fingers over the green flowers on the quilt, watching the shadows on the fabric and the line of her wedding band against her skin. "I saw what it meant to Malcolm when we pulled up to Dunmykel. I wasn't quite prepared for what it would mean to me."

"Odd the hold places can have on one."

She looked up at him in surprise.

Raoul tucked a strand of Emily's red-blonde hair behind her ear. "I can't claim it means to me what it means to you and Malcolm. But I can't deny there are ways it feels like home. And I'm someone who's been used to not having a home for so long I'd have sworn I don't know the meaning of the word."

Mélanie studied her former spymaster across the nursery beds as he stroked Emily's hair. The night light warmed his skin and smoothed away the shadows. She saw him for a moment, hidden in the underbrush, pistol in hand. Or giving her details of a mission in a Spanish mud hut. Then she had a vivid memory of a night in the villa in Italy. The children had all been sick with a fever that had been as intense as fortunately it proved short lived and all the adults had been up and down constantly. One night, Mélanie had come into the night nursery to find Raoul sprawled asleep in a chair with Emily and Jessica sleeping draped over his chest. "I never thought—"

"That you'd see me this way?" He looked at the sleeping children and grinned. "Nor did I. But then, I've always tried to adapt to the needs of the moment." His face went still, the way it sometimes did. "I'm still the man I was, *querida*."

"Meaning you'll be off to Spain again and forget all about us?"

"I'd never forget about any of you, as I think you know. And I'll be back."

She remembered his last letter from Spain, the urgency and excitement behind the crisp words. "You must miss it."

"At times." His gaze was as hooded as ever but uncharacteristically open. She'd learned to recognize those moments when she was his agent. They were still rare, but not nearly so rare as they'd been then. "And when I'm there I miss here. I wasn't lying when I said good spies don't have ties. They also don't make the best fathers."

23

"Malcolm might disagree with that."

"Malcolm stopped being a spy."

"I mean because you were a spy and his father."

Raoul went still for a moment. "Even putting the best possible construction on it, I should have been there more."

"As I understand it, you were there more than a lot of acknowledged fathers."

His mouth twisted. "Whatever my past failures, I'm trying not to fail now. I'm not sure I'm succeeding."

Mélanie laughed. "I once told Bel failing is inevitable when one tries to juggle being a parent with—everything else." For a moment she saw her friend Isobel Lydgate, remembered writing out cards of invitation with her and poring over seating arrangements. "Whether it's being a spy or being a political hostess. Or both. The trick is not minding when you do fail."

Raoul gave another smile. "An excellent point. You've been coping with far more than I have for far longer. Not the first time I've wondered at your abilities."

"I haven't been a field agent for years. Not properly. That's much harder. If—"

She broke off. Across the beds, the tautness of Raoul's shoulders told her he had heard it as well. A stir, a thud, nothing as obvious as footsteps, but a sense that someone was moving in the passage outside. In two seconds, they were both at the door. "Your instincts are as good as ever," Raoul murmured as he eased the door open.

"Being a mother is good for honing them." She cast a quick glance back at the children. None of them stirred.

Raoul pulled the door open enough to peer out into the passage.

It was in shadow, lit only by a faint wash of moonlight from the tall windows at the end. Raoul went still, then they both heard it again. To the right. They slipped down the passage and rounded the corner from the north wing into the central block to see a shadowy form emerging from one of the rooms. The suite that had been Arabella Rannoch's and was still kept empty. Raoul leapt forwards and landed on the intruder in a flying tackle. A report rang through the air. Mélanie felt a sting in her shoulder. The world spun.

Only when she slid to the floor did she realize she'd been shot.

Chapter 4

She came back to shouts and pounding feet. An "I've got him," from Harry, a "*Querida*—" from Raoul, a "Mel—" from Malcolm, his voice sharper than she'd ever heard it.

"I'm all right." She struggled to sit up. "The intruder—"

"Harry and Andrew've gone after him." Malcolm tightened his arm round her. "I'm getting your medical box."

"It's just a scrape."

"Hold still, *querida*." Raoul's face came into view above her, white as bleached linen. "If I'd had a grain of sense—"

Mélanie twisted her head to look him directly in the eye. "Don't you dare blame yourself for my getting winged on a mission. In the old days you wouldn't have thought twice about it."

"In the old days, I was at great pains not to let you see how worried I was." He reached across the passage and ran his fingers over the paneling. "The bullet's buried in the woodwork. So it's not as bad as it might have been."

Malcolm pushed himself to his feet. "Don't let her move. I'm getting her medical box."

But Cordelia came into the passage carrying the box before he could go more than two steps. "Here. I'm not Mélanie, but she's trained me passably well. The children are fine," she added. "They slept through it. Laura's with them, and Gisèle's gone to reassure Strathdon."

"All right," Mélanie said, "I admit it needs bandaging, but for heaven's sake let's go to where there's better light."

Malcolm helped her to her feet and half carried her to their bedchamber. She should perhaps have protested, but in truth the support was welcome. Inside the bedchamber, he pressed her into a chair, dropped a kiss on her hair, and lit a brace of candles and two lamps. By their light, her wound was revealed to be more than a scrape but not serious enough to require stitches. "Go see what Harry and Andrew have found," Mélanie told her husband.

Malcolm shook his head. He had the hand on her uninjured side folded between both his own. "I'm not moving."

Raoul picked up one of the lamps. "I'll go."

Mélanie sucked in her breath as Cordy cleaned the wound with whisky. Really, she was getting soft. She'd been far more badly injured a score of times in the past and scarcely admitted to the pain. Malcolm didn't say anything, but his fingers tightened round her own.

"Sorry," Cordy murmured.

"You're doing splendidly. More light handed than I am."

Cordy was just knotting off the bandage when Raoul returned with Harry and Andrew. None of the three looked happy. "Lost him." Harry's voice was harsh with regret. "He ran into the secret passage off the library. The panel was open so he must have come in that way. We weren't that far behind, but he shot at the ceiling and brought down a hail of rock."

"But he'd already shot me," Mélanie said. "Did he stop and reload his pistol?"

"He had a second," Harry said.

"Good God." It was rare for even a thief to carry one pistol, let alone two.

"His footprints show he took the path to the beach," Andrew said. "But by the time we got to the beach, he was gone."

"So it's someone who knew the house," Cordelia said.

"Yes." Malcolm's voice was grim.

"He came out of Arabella's room," Raoul said. "I doubt that was a random choice, if it's someone who knew the house."

Malcolm nodded. And because no one, very much including Mélanie, was prepared to be left out, they all proceeded down the passage and into the central block, across from the stairs, to the suite that had been Arabella Rannoch's for so many years.

The rooms were done in white and blue and must, Mélanie thought, have been a perfect setting for the golden-haired Arabella Rannoch. Mélanie had only been in them a handful of times, but they had always been kept in meticulous order. Now, the light of the lamp Raoul held revealed the drawers of the dressing table and escritoire pulled from their hinges, the wardrobe gaping open, sheets of yellowed notepaper and gowns not disturbed for years tossed on the floor and bed.

"What the devil were they looking for?" Andrew asked.

"Hard to tell," Malcolm said, though Mélanie knew there were things her husband couldn't share with Andrew, who didn't know about the Elsinore League, the shadowy group begun by Malcolm's putative father Alistair Rannoch, which his mother Arabella had made it her quest to bring down.

"And hard to tell if he found it and was on his way out, or if he'd given up and was going to check another part of the house when we found him," Raoul said.

They moved to the adjoining dressing room, which was in a similar state. The intruder had even taken a knife to the chaise-longue cushions. Mélanie felt a jolt of rage run through her husband.

"Do you notice anything missing, Andrew?" Harry asked, as they moved round the room.

Andrew shook his head. "But it's difficult to know without knowing what they were looking for. So far as I know, there's nothing of particular value left in these rooms. Gelly and Lady Frances and Lady Marjorie have all of Lady Arabella's jewelry." They divided in pairs to make a quick circuit of the rest of the rooms, but no other room showed signs of disturbance. "So he started with Arabella's rooms," Raoul said. "And either found what he wanted—in which case it was something small enough to tuck into his coat—or left without finding it."

"Does that mean he'll be back?" Andrew asked.

"Very likely," Malcolm said. "If he didn't find it."

Andrew gave a quick nod. He'd lived his life at Dunmykel, with a few years as an Edinburgh lawyer, but Mélanie knew he'd seen enough of Malcolm's work through the years not to be surprised. "I'll update Gelly and the duke," he said.

Which was prudent, and also a way of letting the rest of them talk freely.

"Andrew's always been the soul of tact," Malcolm said when his friend left his and Mélanie's bedchamber, to which they had all adjourned. "Gelly's likely to have more questions."

Mélanie looked into the night nursery. The children were all still asleep. Laura got up from the edge of Emily and Livia's bed and crossed to Mélanie's side. "You're being impossibly stoic, aren't you?"

"Nonsense. It's only a flesh wound." Mélanie's smiled brightly, her arm held still to minimize the pull on her shoulder.

"As I said." Laura echoed the smile, but there was a line between her brows.

27

Malcolm had poked up the banked fire and was staring into the grate when she and Laura returned to the room, but he moved to her side at once and put his arm round her, carefully, so as not to jar her wound.

"I'm all right, darling." She smiled into his eyes, though in truth her shoulder stung like the devil.

"A few inches over and that bullet could have nicked your lung. We've been on British soil less than twenty-four hours, and you've been shot."

"But even you have to admit the break-in couldn't have had anything to do with our being here."

"Someone could have known we'd left Italy. Carfax almost certainly does. We know he's been watching us." Malcolm's gaze darkened, and Mélanie felt again the restless tension that had coiled through him for the whole of their journey.

"But the intruder was in Lady Arabella's rooms," Cordy said. She was sitting on the settee, blonde hair spilling over her shoulders, her dressing gown a froth of rose silk and white lace about her. "That doesn't sound as though it's anything to do with you."

"No," Malcolm agreed. He drew Mélanie over to a wingback chair and perched on the arm. "And anyone who knew about the secret passage would probably know the layout of the house. In any case, Mama's rooms wouldn't be the logical place to start a random search." He looked at Raoul, who had gone to lean against the back of the chair where Laura was sitting.

"There are any number of people who might have reason to be interested in information Arabella possessed," Raoul said. "Starting with the Elsinore League. But it's difficult to determine why now. Especially for the League. Until Alistair died a year and a half ago, this was his house. He could have torn it apart whenever he liked."

"Quite." Malcolm rested a hand, again lightly, on Mélanie's uninjured shoulder. "I'd say they were more likely to be searching for something of Alistair's, save that it's difficult to imagine something of Alistair's being in Arabella's rooms."

"Unless he hid it there after she died," Laura suggested. "He'd have known those rooms were little used."

Malcolm shot her an appreciative look. "That's possible. And might have appealed to Alistair's twisted sense of humor."

"We know the League know about the secret passage," Harry said. It was one thing they had learned from his uncle Archie in Italy in the autumn. That there were secret rooms off the secret passage where the League had indulged in parties, more given to their cover as a hellfire club than to their actual mission of manipulating international events to their advantage.

Malcolm's mouth tightened. The rooms had a warped Shakespearean theme. Mélanie knew they particularly bothered him. "True," he said. "But there's still the question of why *now*. Alistair's death is more recent than Arabella's, but it's been a year and a half. What's changed?"

"We have the list of names of League members," Mélanie said. Retrieving that list had been a lucky triumph of their investigation in September. "Something they're afraid of our seeing because we now know who's an Elsinore League member?"

She saw a flash of worry in Malcolm's gaze, because that tied the break-in back to their arrival. "It's possible," he said, with the neutrality of an agent. "Though, if Arabella had something so vital to use against the League, why hide it away?"

"The Elsinore League are obvious suspects," Raoul said, "but not the only ones. Any of Arabella's lovers might have reason to recover papers she left. And like the Elsinore League members, they might know about the secret passage."

Malcolm met his father's gaze. "Do you know—"

"Their names? Some, but certainly not all. Many have links to the League, but a number don't. But again, one wonders why they'd suddenly be interested in something in her possession now."

"Or Carfax could be interested in anything Arabella had relating to the Elsinore League." Malcolm spoke in the same neutral voice, but his fingers were taut against Mélanie's back. "He knows we have the list too."

"But if he knew, or even suspected, that your mother had hidden anything here relating to the Elsinore League," Harry said, "you'd think he also would have searched years ago."

"True," Malcolm said. "Carfax has even been a guest here himself, and it certainly wouldn't be difficult for him to have an agent infiltrate the house or break in. Which again makes the question of 'why now' interesting."

Mélanie shifted her position in the chair, felt a stab of fire through her shoulder, tried to control her indrawn breath. "Our coming to Dunmykel is certainly significant. But perhaps we're wrong to look at everything revolving round us. Perhaps there's something else that makes whatever the intruder was searching for significant now."

"And it's coincidence the break-in happened the night we arrived?" Malcolm's arm shifted round her, and she saw a flash of concern in his eyes.

She squeezed his hand to let him know she was all right. "I hate coincidence as much as you do, darling. But it does occur."

Harry stretched his legs out in front of him. "Who else would have known about the secret passage?"

"The servants," Malcolm said. "Various guests who've stayed here through the years, though not all. Some of the tenants." He went still, and when Mélanie twisted her head round to look up at him she saw he was frowning. "Smugglers have been using the caves off the beach, at the end of the secret passage for years. Andrew more or less turns a blind eye to them, especially those disrupted by Alistair's clearances." Malcolm had worked hard to overturn the damage Alistair had done since he'd inherited the estate, but many of the tenants were still in difficult circumstances.

"What if—" Mélanie's gaze locked on her husband's, as so often when they were piecing possibilities together. "If the smugglers wanted to hide something in the house, Arabella's rooms would be a good choice, as they aren't used much. Then, when we returned, they might have worried whatever it was wasn't safe."

An answering glint kindled in Malcolm's eyes. "That's the most probable theory we've hit on so far, Mel. Though whatever it is would have to be small if the intruder took it. And if it's still there, I'm at a loss as to where it might be hidden. Which doesn't mean it's not there. I'll talk to Andrew tomorrow." He cast a glance round the company. "I think we're safe for tonight, especially since Andrew, Harry, and Raoul blocked access from the passage into the library. But tomorrow we should set a watch."

"Just in case things might start to seem dull," Cordelia said with a bright smile.

Malcolm met her gaze. "Quite."

Chapter 5

Strathdon clunked his coffee cup down on a silver tray. "Someone *shot* Suz—Mélanie?"

"He was firing off a warning shot, not aiming for her, I think, but yes." Malcolm kept his voice even with an effort.

Strathdon stared at Malcolm across the rich red and gold of the Turkey rug in his room. "Does this mean you're going to be off at once?"

That had been Malcolm's first impulse, holding his bleeding wife in his arms, but he now knew it was no answer. "Leaving you and Gelly and Andrew to deal with the consequences? No, I think it means we have all the more reason to stay for the present. We have to make sure there are no further break-ins. And learn what it was the man was after."

"Something of Arabella's."

"Seemingly."

Strathdon settled back in his chair and reached for his coffee. "The smugglers have been using the secret passage for years. Hiding goods in the house at times, I shouldn't wonder. I suppose you're going to talk to Andrew about that."

Malcolm met his grandfather's gaze. "The less you know, the better, Grandfather."

Strathdon took a sip of coffee. "For once, I quite agree with you."

Andrew was wrapping a garland round the stair rail in the great hall when Malcolm was able to snatch a moment from the cheerful chaos of a house full of young children to talk to him alone.

Andrew looked up from twining the garland round the half-landing newel post to greet Malcolm with a grin. "It's a bit early, but I thought we should get these up for Jessica's birthday tomorrow. I understand Mélanie's given Mrs. Gordon instructions about the cake."

"Chocolate with dried cherries." Despite the break-in and the uncertainty about Strathdon's plans, Mélanie's focus today was all on Jessica's birthday. It was, she had pointed out, one thing they could control.

"I have the footmen and grooms set to keep watch in shifts tonight," Andrew said, his face going serious. "With you and me and Davenport and O'Roarke, we should be covered without anyone needing to stay up all night."

"Not to mention Mel and Cordy, and probably Laura, unless she can be persuaded to sleep because of the baby. Thank you, Andrew." Malcolm picked up the free end of the garland and wrapped it round the stair rail going down from the half-landing. "Do the smugglers still use the caves off the secret passage?"

He said it abruptly on purpose. Even with a friend like Andrew, it was often a good tactic to try to catch a person off guard. Perhaps especially so when the ties of friendship could cut against his instincts.

Andrew went still. "Malcolm—"

"There are things I prefer not to know. Quite right. But last night's events changed things."

Andrew's brows drew together. "You think smugglers—"

"Could any of them have been using my mother's rooms to store something?"

"My God, Malcolm, you saw how the rooms were torn apart. If you imagine anyone could have hidden crates of brandy or bolts of silk in there—"

"No. But something smaller? We both know that when Alistair was alive, some of the smugglers round here ferried works of art from the Continent for him. Works that even now adorn the house." Malcolm's gaze went to the grisaille paintings of the Nine Muses that lined the pine-wainscoted stair wall. He was quite sure Alistair hadn't acquired them through legal channels.

"You think someone hid an art treasure in your mother's rooms—"

"And then decided to retrieve it when we arrived. At least it's one explanation. The most probable of an improbable set of them."

"Whoever searched the rooms isn't the person who hid it," Andrew said. "Unless they have a very poor memory."

"A good point. But a smuggler could still have hidden something. Perhaps something he was keeping from his fellows. And another could have realized it was there."

Andrew tightened the garland, his gaze thoughtful. "I can make some inquiries. The men are loyal to the family overall. If someone broke in, he won't be popular. Certainly not if he broke in with pistols and fired at Mélanie." Andrew plucked a brown needle from the garland. "Most of the men don't go armed."

"No," Malcolm said, "I know it. But I also know the local lads have been known to make alliances with some less than savory elements." Such as some larger smuggling operations in the south. He and Mélanie had tangled with one of them on one of their visits. It would be a long time before Malcolm entirely got past his wife's being held at gunpoint. "Go carefully, Andrew."

Andrew's gaze showed the same memories were in his mind. "Oh, believe me, I will." He surveyed Malcolm for a moment down the length of pine-garlanded stair rail. "It's good to have you back."

"It's good to be back." That was true, more so than he wanted to admit. More so than he was going to admit to anyone, especially his wife and grandfather.

Andrew smoothed a length of red ribbon wound round the garland. "We've done our best to deflect talk."

"And not asked questions. You're a good fellow, Andrew."

Andrew gave a crooked grin. "I've known you had secrets since you were at Oxford. And I'm perhaps a bit more patient than Gelly. Needless to say, you're missed. By everyone at Dunmykel."

Malcolm took a step down the stairs, twining the garland as he went. "That's kind of you, Andrew. But you've been running the estate for years. Gelly knows more about it now than I do."

"It's amazing how she's taken to it." Andrew followed, adjusting the garland as he went. "I used to worry she wouldn't be happy immured in the country—"

"You worry too much, Andrew." Malcolm tugged a length of garland tighter. "You worried too much about marrying Gelly, in particular."

"If you mean I was aware I'm thirteen years older and she has five times my birth and fortune—"

"More or less." Malcolm backed down another step. "As I recall, I had to give you my consent before you asked for it. And encourage you to speak to Alistair." It had been an uncomfortable conversation, though

Alistair had consented surprisingly readily. Perhaps because he knew Gisèle wasn't his biological daughter. Perhaps, Malcolm thought, because despite that he was fond of her.

"For which I'm eternally grateful," Andrew said. "But whatever Gelly and I do for Dunmykel, don't ever make the mistake of thinking you don't matter. You have the perspective of having grown up here—"

"So do you."

"It's not the same." Andrew paused on the step above, gaze locked on Malcolm's own. "It's your estate."

"For God's sake, Andrew. That makes a mockery of everything we both believe in. And in any case, we both know it's laughable to say it's in my blood."

"No, but it means something to the tenants." Andrew cast a brief glance over the stair rail at the great hall, the marble tiles, the framed royal charter that hung casually in one corner, the crossed swords over the fireplace. Malcolm suspected he was picturing Boxing Day and other festivals when the house was thrown open to the tenants and villagers. "You can argue all you want in Parliament against the landed class, but you can't deny what it means here on the ground. Even to those who'd be quick to join Radical societies. Even to those who want things to change—and God knows there are plenty of them in Scotland—seeing you here, working for that change, is a reminder of what's possible."

Malcolm kept his gaze steady on his childhood friend's. "You're saying I ran from my responsibilities for ten years and I'm doing so again."

"Christ, Malcolm. I'd never put it that way. You're much too hard on yourself for me to ever say anything of the kind. I understand why you've stayed away. And Dunmykel wasn't yours then."

"No, it was Alistair's." Alistair's portrait was gone from the great hall, but Alistair's art treasures still filled the house. "And his enclosures did incalculable damage."

"Which you undid as much as you could when the estate became yours. Don't think the tenants aren't aware of that. It's why they trust you."

Malcolm curled his fingers round the stair rail. The pine prickled his hand. Whatever Andrew might say now, Malcolm knew his staying away in the decade after he left university had hurt his friend. And though Malcolm might have been at odds—to put it mildly—with Alistair, his presence as the heir would have meant something to the tenants. "It's not ideal. But I've had time for them to know me, at least. They know you're enacting policies we've agreed on—"

"On which I could use your input. I'm a decent estate agent, Malcolm. Better than I thought I'd be in my father's day, when I thought I could never live up to him. But never think I don't need your input. You saw what it meant when we strategized about putting up cottages in the south meadow."

"And we can do it again. It's not as though we can't see each other, Andrew. Or write, of course. But I hope you and Gelly and Ian will come back to Italy soon."

"Of course we will, if it's the only way to see you." Andrew studied him for a long moment. "I know you, Malcolm. I know you wouldn't stay away from your responsibilities if you didn't feel you had to. I want you to know you're missed. And also that I understand just how serious this must be. If there's any way I can help you—"

Malcolm gripped his oldest friend's arm. "I can't thank you enough, Andrew."

"But you won't let me help."

"Andrew, if I could—"

"It's all right, Malcolm. That is, I understand. We went separate ways when I went to Edinburgh and you went to Oxford. I know I don't move in your world. It doesn't change my wanting you back. For Gelly's sake. For the tenants' sake. And for my own."

Mélanie tied a pink satin ribbon round the waist of the doll that was Jessica's main birthday present.

"She's young for a china-headed doll," Malcolm said, looking up from fastening the wheels on a doll carriage they had packed in pieces.

"She's careful." Mélanie tweaked the doll's curly dark hair. She had ordered her by post from her modiste friend Marthe, complete with her gown of pink gauze and satin and long white gloves, but Mélanie, Cordy, and Laura had made her pearl bandeau, pleated silk fan, and satin-lined velvet evening cloak themselves. "This way she can play with the older girls. And we can start building a collection for her."

She caught Malcolm's quick smile, and knew he was thinking that she was assuming a settled life for them. But really, something in their lives had to be stable. Why not the children's toys?

Malcolm cast a glance towards the cradle where Jessica was sound asleep. "I can't believe she's turning two. It seems like her first birthday was just yesterday—"

He sucked in his breath. A year ago, on Jessica's first birthday, they had just been beginning to put their marriage together after he learned she'd been a French spy. For a while, she hadn't been sure they'd have the party at all. In the end, they'd been closer by Jessica's birthday than she'd dreamed possible when he learned the truth, but still miles away from where they were today. They'd only cautiously begun to resume a physical relationship, and though they'd recovered kindness, emotional intimacy had still seemed out of reach. Raoul had been a guest at the party, invited by Malcolm—to Mélanie's amazement—but he'd hardly seemed like one of the family. She remembered his laughing with Laura at one point, but they'd barely been friends, let alone lovers. And of course they'd been in the Berkeley Square house.

"It's been quite a year," she said.

Malcolm set down the screwdriver and crossed to her side. "Even then I remember marveling at my happiness."

"Darling. I thought our rule was to try to be honest."

"I am being honest. How could I have looked at you and Jessica and Colin and not been happy?"

"We'd just—"

"Almost lost everything. I was still adjusting, but I had enough sense to appreciate what we had." He stroked his fingers against her cheek. "But that was nothing compared to how happy I am now."

Despite everything they'd lost. Despite the ache that was still there at the back of his eyes, and that she knew always would be. She leaned her cheek against his hand. "A year ago, I couldn't believe what we had. And yet what we have now seemed as distant as the moon."

He bent his head and kissed her. She tangled her fingers in his hair, but when he lifted his head she saw a quizzical light in his eyes. "What?" she asked.

"I'm remembering Harry talking to us at Jessica's first birthday. He knew then. Or guessed."

Mélanie saw Harry proposing a toast to Jessica as she and Malcolm cautiously negotiated the new terrain of their marriage. "I always knew Harry was a good friend," she said. "But until the past six months, I don't think I realized quite how good."

"Something else to be grateful for." He leaned in and kissed her again. "I should be off. I told Andrew I'd be part of the first watch."

She slid her fingers behind his neck and held him to her for a moment. "You'll wake me for the second watch."

"Word of honor." He brushed his lips across her forehead. "Even if honor is but a word."

"All clear, so far." Harry came up the stairs and stopped beside Malcolm, who was keeping watch on the first-floor landing. "The footmen and grooms seem like sensible lads. Of course, one can never really have everything covered."

"Quite," Malcolm said. He cast a glance down the passage towards the north wing, the night nursery and their bedchamber, where he profoundly hoped Mélanie was managing to sleep. "Mel made me promise to wake her for the next watch."

"Cordy too." Harry hesitated. "She also said, worrying as it was, it was rather a relief to be able to take direct action."

Malcolm gave a reluctant grin. "I confess I'm not immune to that myself. Much as I wish this hadn't happened, it does make waiting for Grandfather's plan somewhat easier."

Footsteps sounded below. Malcolm tensed and felt Harry do the same. But then the light of the wall sconces caught Andrew's dark hair.

"Sorry," Andrew said, stopping beside them. "But I've someone below Malcolm should talk to."

"Go," Harry said. "I've got things here."

Without further explanation, Andrew led Malcolm down the stairs and into the library, the only part of the original thirteenth-century keep to have been incorporated into the current house. The air always smelled different here, as though it, too, had absorbed the history of the room. Malcolm felt his throat tighten. This had been his favorite room at Dunmykel as a child. But now he could not step over the threshold without remembering it was where his mother had put a bullet through her brain.

The light of the candle Andrew carried fell over the fireplace, the tall ranks of bookshelves, the high-backed chairs. Andrew had already moved the gateleg table he, Harry, and Raoul had used to block the secret passage. He pressed the bend in the griffin's tail on the Rannoch coat of arms carved into one of the pilasters that flanked the fireplace. A bookcase slid back to reveal the passage.

Chapter 6

Malcolm ducked his head beneath the low lintel and followed Andrew into the dirt-floored, granite-walled passage they had so often explored as boys. A pile of debris a few feet down showed where the intruder had shot rock from the ceiling to delay Harry. The passage branched off further down, with one path leading to the book room in the lodge. The sixteenth century lord of the manor who had had the passage built had been having an affair with the steward's wife. Andrew's father had been the estate agent at Dunmykel and had lived at the lodge with his family. The passage had been a convenient way to communicate when Malcolm and Andrew were boys. And later, to slip out of Dunmykel quietly when Malcolm needed to catch a boat. For the other branch of the passage led to the caves off the beach.

Andrew took the path to the caves. Malcolm caught a whiff of salt air over the damp and rock of the passage. The rumble of the sea cut the stillness. They rounded a bend and saw a faint glow of light ahead, as though from a lantern, spilling onto the granite walls of the passage. They emerged into a wide cave. Off to the side was the carving that, he now knew, concealed the second sliding panel that led to the Elsinore League's rooms. Alistair's rooms. He'd searched them earlier in the day in case they contained any clues to the break-in. He hadn't found anything, but he now knew that in addition to bawdy Shakespearean murals, the rooms contained multiple beds, crystal glasses, stage props, and fancy dress. Not to mention handcuffs and birch rods.

Malcolm forced his gaze away. Because that wasn't Andrew's destination. In the main cave, a shadowy figure was leaning against a stack of crates, lit by a single lantern set in a niche in the wall. His face was in darkness, but Malcolm recognized the easy way he held himself.

"Stephen," Malcolm said. "I trust Alice and the children are well."

MIDWINTER INTRIGUE

Stephen Drummond had explored the beach and caves with Malcolm and Andrew when they were all boys, and smuggled ale out of his father's inn to share with them on fishing expeditions. Now he was married and the father of three, running the Griffin & Dragon inn himself. But the depredations of Alistair's clearances had also driven him to work with the smugglers, as Malcolm had learned the previous year.

"They are." Stephen stepped forwards and extended his hand. "And it's good to see you back."

Malcolm clasped Stephen's hand and flung an arm round his shoulders. "It's a quiet visit, or—"

"I understand. And that's not what we're here to talk about in any case."

Malcolm scanned his childhood friend's face. Stephen was a good man, a loyal friend and husband and father. But Malcolm knew only too well what desperate men could be driven to. Stephen probably knew the house better than any of the tenants and villagers. "Do you know anything about what happened last night?"

"I'm not the one who broke in, if that's what you mean. I'm not saying I'd never use the passage for the right reason, but I wouldn't fire a pistol, certainly not anywhere near Mrs. Rannoch."

Malcolm released his breath. "I didn't think you were."

"But you had to ask. It's all right, we're not the lads we were. Our interests don't always align. But I'll always be loyal to this family." Stephen hesitated a moment. "I'll always be loyal to you."

"That's good of you. And not necessarily deserved, given my absence."

"God, Malcolm, you're my friend. And you've done more for Dunmykel than you realize. Alistair's actions can't be undone in a day." Stephen cast a glance over his shoulder at Andrew, who was hanging back. "As I told Andrew, I didn't break in last night, and I don't know of anything any of the lads were hiding in the house. I'm not saying we haven't stored the odd extra crate in the cellars on occasion, but not lately, and we've certainly never used Lady Arabella's rooms, or any of the upstairs rooms, come to that. But as I told Andrew, there's been a man about, looking to hire one of the lads for a job."

"What sort of job?"

"He didn't say. Or at least I don't know that he did. I only heard about it because Alice's younger brother got wind of it, and asked me what I thought, and I told him he was a damned fool if he even considered getting involved. Apparently the man had a London accent.

Or that's how it was described, which could mean anyone from the south. I thought it was a rival to Wheaton, looking to cut in on the local trade. Just wanted to keep my friends and family well out of it. But when Andrew told me about last night, it cast a different light on it."

"Do you know who might have agreed?"

Stephen shook his head. "I can ask about a bit more."

"Thank you. But go carefully. We don't know quite what we're up against."

Stephen gave a slow nod. "It isn't like any of the lads to go armed. Not with two pistols, especially."

"That was my thinking," Andrew said.

"Perhaps the job was just getting this man from the south into the house," Malcolm said. "Do you have a description of him?"

"I've been doing my best to assemble details. Middle years—which, given that most of the lads who talked to him are barely out of their teens, could mean anything from our age to sixties. Dark hair worn a bit long. Eyes that were brown or gray or blue depending on who's telling the story. Tall, thin. Walked with slightly hunched shoulders. Dresses 'like a gentleman'—which again could mean a lot of things."

"You have a knack for this," Malcolm said.

Stephen shrugged. "Seemed the least I could do." He hesitated a moment, shifting his weight from one foot to the other. "There's one other thing. I'm not sure it means much, because it came from Sam Macdonald, and he's never been further south than Perth. But, while everyone else said the man sounded as if he were 'from the south,' Sam thought he was a Frenchman."

"The man who broke in is French?" Cordelia asked. They were gathered in Malcolm and Mélanie's room—Cordelia, Harry, Malcolm, Mélanie, Raoul, and Laura—while Andrew and the footmen and grooms handled the watch. Malcolm had just updated them on his talk with Stephen.

"One man out of a half dozen who met him thought so," Malcolm said. "As Stephen said, it could mean nothing at all. But it is interesting." He looked across the room at his father.

"Surely you aren't asking if I hired one of the local lads to break in and search for something in Arabella's rooms," Raoul said. "Besides, I wouldn't seem French."

MIDWINTER INTRIGUE

"Not unless you tried to, in which case you could fool a Frenchman," Malcolm said. "But I was wondering if Mama could have hidden anything that would interest anyone French."

"Royalists? Or Bonapartists?"

"Either."

"Your mother's focus was always the Elsinore League. She knew about my work in France, but we never shared it."

"No, I know. At least, I don't know that you shared it. But when it comes to Arabella—not to mention you—there's still a great deal I don't know."

Raoul didn't flinch from his gaze. "Fair enough. But I know of no particular involvement Arabella had in France. Except that Alistair and others in the League were in and out of France a great deal in the eighties and nineties."

"And Alistair, Dewhurst, and Smytheton were Royalist agents."

"So they were." Raoul's brows drew together in consideration.

"It couldn't—I know it sounds mad, but it couldn't be Julien St. Juste, could it?" Cordelia asked.

"Julien wouldn't seem French unless he wanted to, any more than Raoul would," Mélanie said. "Of course knowing Julien, he could adopt a French accent to put us off our guard." She drew her knees up on the settee and locked her arms over her seafoam dressing gown. Her movements were deliberately casual, but Malcolm caught the way she was favoring her shoulder. "I don't quite see how even Julien could manage to look tall, though."

Malcolm turned his gaze back to his father. "Did Arabella have a French—"

"Lover?" Raoul finished, in a matter-of-fact voice. "Several. I don't see any particular connection to the break-in, though."

"Someone who was French or seemed French could have been working for anyone," Harry said. "The Elsinore League. Carfax. Given the number of émigrés in London, it doesn't even have to be someone from abroad."

"A good point," Malcolm said. "But whether he's French or not, we seem to have an outsider who came here in search of something. Which he believes is hidden in Arabella's rooms. God, I wish Aunt Frances was here."

"She will be within the week," Mélanie said. "Perhaps even tomorrow. She said they'd try to arrive for Jessica's birthday."

41

"Meanwhile, we'll have to hope Stephen can learn more. And I can talk to Grandfather. He knows more of what's going on in his children's lives than he lets on."

For the second morning in a row, Strathdon surveyed Malcolm over his steaming cup of coffee, rare shock in his blue eyes. "You're telling me a French spy broke into the house to steal something of Arabella's?"

"Not precisely." Malcolm was leaning against the window in his grandfather's room, hands braced on the sill. "Or at least not necessarily, though I suppose that is one possible theory. Someone who may be French broke into the house to steal something of Arabella's. Or at least something he believed hidden in Arabella's rooms."

Strathdon's brows snapped together. "I long since accepted that there's a great deal about Arabella I didn't know. But I don't believe—"

"That she was spying for the French?" Malcolm said in a level voice. "No one else does either. But her investigation into the Elsinore League took her into France. For that matter, she was half French herself."

"If you're suggesting this has something to do with your grandmother—"

"I wouldn't have thought so, but I've learned not to discount anything."

Malcolm's grandmother, the Duchess of Strathdon, had been born Louise de Lisle. She had died before Malcolm was born, when Arabella was still in her teens. Strathdon rarely talked about her. But he kept her portrait in his rooms. He had never, to Malcolm's knowledge, come close to remarrying, and if he had kept a mistress he was very discreet.

"Your grandmother was a brilliant woman, but it's difficult to imagine anything of hers that could interest a thief now, beyond the obvious value of jewels."

Some members of the de Lisle family had settled in Britain during the Revolution. Others had remained in France and done quite well for themselves. But none, Malcolm agreed, had had particular links to Arabella.

"Is there anything you can imagine Mama might have hidden?"

MIDWINTER INTRIGUE

"Any number of things. Letters to a lover. Letters she wanted to leave for you children. Information she'd uncovered in this never-ending quest of hers. But if you're asking if I remember anything specific, then no."

Malcolm nodded, pushed himself away from the sill, and touched his grandfather on the shoulder. "We won't solve it all at once. Come downstairs and enjoy your great-granddaughter's birthday."

"I can't believe she's still awake. And so cheerful." Gisèle looked to the middle of the old drawing room where Jessica was perched on the carpet, surrounded by a litter of paper and ribbon, dragging a comb through the hair of her new doll. Emily and Livia had brought three other dolls downstairs and were setting up a tea party. Colin was pouring tea from a china pot. Good God, Laura and Mel had managed to pack a lot of toys, Malcolm thought.

The adults were gathered round, disposed on the cream silk sofas and canvaswork chairs, leaning against the walls, sipping champagne and mulled wine. Malcolm and Gisèle's aunt Frances had arrived earlier in the day along with her new husband, Archibald Davenport, Harry's uncle, and her youngest daughter Chloe.

"The children have always stayed up late and slept late," Malcolm told his sister. "And Jessica's old enough to understand what her birthday is. She doesn't want to sleep through a minute." A year ago she'd taken a nap in Mel's arms in the midst of it. "Thank you," Malcolm said to his sister. "It's a splendid birthday party, though I know you had to put it together at the last minute."

"When you wrote you were coming, I hoped you'd be here for her birthday. Andrew and I missed the first one."

Malcolm's touched his sister's arm. "That's one benefit to all this."

Gisèle drew a breath, glanced at Strathdon, presiding over the scene from a wingback chair, and looked back at Malcolm. "I'm sorry. I hated lying to you. I hated making you worry. But you know what Grandfather's like when he's determined about something."

Malcolm studied his little sister. He'd been abroad for far too much of her childhood. And now they were once again living on the Continent. It had taken him a while on his return to properly realize she

43

was no longer a child. But he'd come to appreciate the woman she'd grown into. "I do. And I also know just how formidable you are."

Gisèle folded her arms across her chest. "Against Grandfather—"

"Against anyone."

Gisèle glanced away. "Damn it, Malcolm. You finally seemed to have put down roots here. You were happy in Parliament, I'd swear it. You were even happy in the Berkeley Square house, as hard as that once was to imagine. Then you go off to the Continent—in the middle of the night, as best I can make out—leaving a letter that's a non-explanation but that more or less implies you may never come back." She turned back to him. "You don't think I had questions? That I wanted my brother back?"

Malcolm's throat went tight with words he couldn't speak. He'd more than half expected Gelly to ask such questions in Italy, but the focus had been on Frances and Archie's wedding, and Gisèle had been determinedly cheerful. Of course, at that point there also hadn't been any discussion of a plan for them to return. "Gelly, you have to know that if I felt we needed to leave—"

"I know." Gisèle fixed him with a hard stare. "Your mysterious work and saving the country and secrets you can't share with me. I've been hearing that since I was ten years old. But I'm not a child anymore."

"You must forgive an elder brother's slowness, but I know full well you aren't."

Gisèle ran her fingers down the white-painted shutter behind her. Outside, wind battered the mullioned windows, and from the chill leaching through Malcolm suspected it had started to snow. "You told Aunt Frances why you had to leave. Don't pretend you didn't. She was determined to get at the truth when she and Archie and Chloe left for the Continent, and then when we joined you all in Italy for her wedding she seemed perfectly sanguine about the situation."

For a moment, the hurt in her eyes made him at once want to hug her like a child and confess the whole to her like an adult confidante. But the truth put Gisèle—and others—at risk. "For her own sake, I'd prefer Aunt Frances know as little as possible. She learned enough on her own that it forced my hand."

"And she's married to Archie and he's involved in all sorts of secret things while Andrew and I live sadly quiet lives. No." Gisèle put up a hand when he started to protest. "Part of me does understand. But this goes to why I didn't tell you about Grandfather's plan. If I'm to accept your keeping things from me for my own good, you have to accept my doing the same. You can't blame me for thinking it's in your best interest for Grandfather's plan to work."

"Gelly—" Malcolm put out a hand to his sister, but somehow he knew that reaching out to her as he would have when she was younger wouldn't work now. "You saw us in Italy. You must realize we're happy there."

Gisèle leaned against the window, hands braced on the sill. "I'd say you were content. And at the same time, that both you and Suz—Mélanie were starting to get restless. I sometimes find Scotland limiting. I can't believe the two of you can be happy permanently on Lake Como. Or that Raoul can, or Laura, for that matter. Harry might be happy looking at antiquities, but Cordelia will miss society and you'd both miss the Davenports if they left. You can't think me so naïve as to believe this is a long-term solution for anyone."

Malcolm could hear his wife's laughter and an answering whoop from Harry above the children's chatter. Happiness in the moment. It was what he had learned to seize on. "It may not be an ideal solution, but it's one that can work. And there are surprising compensations."

"Damn it, Malcolm." Gisèle crossed to him in two strides and gripped his coat. "You missed most of my childhood. I want my brother back."

His hands closed on her shoulders. "And I want my sister. However I feel about leaving much of our life in Britain, you can't think I have anything but regret at being away from you and Andrew and Ian."

"Well, then." The face she turned up to him was hard with determination and at the same time had the pleading of a very young girl asking to be reassured that fairy tales were real.

"Gelly." His throat was thick. "I'll never forgive myself for being gone so long when you were young. For running away on my own account when you needed me—"

"Stop it, Malcolm. There's too much guilt in this family as it is. And you're prevaricating."

He smiled down at her, though he could feel a traitorous pressure behind his eyes. "We had time in Italy this fall. We'll have more time."

"It's not the same." Gisèle tilted her chin up. "Back here at Dunmykel, you can't tell me being at the villa is the same."

Malcolm shut his senses to the granite and the scent of burning pine and the sea smell that leached into the walls. "You're my sister wherever we are. Andrew's my friend and now my brother. Ian's my nephew. Nothing can change that."

"But this is home. For you, even more than me. You grew up here."

For many years it had been a refuge. For all it was Alistair's, Arabella had left her stamp on it. His parents had rarely been here, and when they were in residence at the same time he was, it was easier to avoid them than in London. That is, to avoid Alistair. Some of his happiest memories of Arabella were here, playing on the beach, at her Broadwood grand pianoforte in this room, devising codes in the library. He had a lot of memories of Raoul here too. Curled up on a window seat reading Shakespeare. Rambles in the woods. Throwing a ball on the lawn. Exploring the Old Tower. "And it always will be," he said. "But home is more about whom one is with than any particular place. If I hadn't already known that, going to Italy proved it to me."

Gisèle looked at the tea party on the hearth rug. Colin now had Jessica in his lap and was helping her pour. Emily was offering a cup of tea to a bemused Berowne and Chloe's puppy. "You have to want the children to grow up—"

"I want the children to grow up happy. And safe."

Gisèle swallowed, her eyes hard on his face. "All the more reason to want Grandfather's plan to work. If the children are at risk, you can't really believe you can keep them safe just by staying in Italy."

Gisèle had nicked a raw nerve. "Gelly, if I believed it could help—"

"I don't see why you can't at least try."

"I am. I'm hearing him out."

"You've already made up your mind. And you're the one who's always told me the importance of keeping an open mind."

Malcolm looked into those blue eyes that he'd never been able to resist, from the moment his mother first put her into his arms as a newborn. "A palpable hit, sister mine. I promise I'll listen. Is that better?"

Gisèle regarded him with a look that suddenly reminded him of their mother. "It's a start."

A shout of laughter cut the tense air between him and his sister. Malcolm glanced down the room. Jessica and Emily were now serving pretend tea to the adults, while Colin and Livia appeared to be assembling plates of pretend cakes. Chloe had joined them. Emily was draping a doll cloak over Berowne. "Let's join the children," he said. "They have a way—"

He broke off as the door opened and Alec, one of the footmen, stepped in. Last night Alec had been in his shirtsleeves, gaze bright with the light of adventure as he helped patrol the house. Now he was back in his green livery. But his gaze still had the alert look of one aware that not all was as it should be in the house. Malcolm and Gisèle moved towards him, and he met them midway across the room. He bowed to Gisèle. "We've had a caller, madam."

Dunmykel was not the sort of place one simply called, particularly in winter with snow falling. Malcolm cast a quick glance at the rest of the company. The children were still playing, but the adults had gone quiet. Mélanie met his gaze for a moment.

"Mr. Oliver Lydgate," the footman continued. "I recognized him and took the liberty of offering to bring him up. But he asked to wait in the library instead. He's asking for Mr. Rannoch."

The doll's tea party continued. The fire still blazed in the grate. But the world had shifted. Malcolm saw the tension that ran through his wife.

Gisèle's brows drew together. Oliver had been a family friend since she was in the nursery, coming and going easily from the various Rannoch houses. In Italy, Malcolm had avoided saying much to her about Oliver and his wife Isobel. Now her gaze went to Malcolm's.

"I'll go down and talk to him," Malcolm said. He met Mélanie's gaze, then glanced at Harry and Raoul, a sort of silent confirmation that they were all on their guard.

It was Cordelia who put what they were all thinking into words. "If Oliver somehow knew you were here—"

"Carfax almost certainly does as well," Malcolm said. "Quite. But then we knew that was likely. The question is, did he send Oliver?"

Chapter 7

Malcolm cast another quick glance at the children before he left the room. Still absorbed in their game. Had he been a fool to come here? Or not to have left the moment he learned his grandfather was well? He told himself they were safe for a short time. That he owed it to his grandfather to at least hear his plan. That it wasn't good for the children to spend the holidays traveling. But the truth was he'd succumbed to the lure of Christmas at Dunmykel himself.

He went down the main staircase, the stair rail now fully garlanded, into the hall, hung with pine bows and red ribbon, and to the library where he and Andrew had gone through the panel and down the secret passage only last night. Now the sliding panel was closed, blocked once again with the gateleg table. A familiar figure stood before the fireplace.

"Oliver." Malcolm closed the library door.

Oliver spun to face him. He still wore his greatcoat, dusted with snow on the shoulders. It was only six months since Malcolm had seen him, but he seemed to have aged far more. He had always had a boyish charm that had seemed unfaded from Oxford to the halls of Westminster a decade later, but now the bones of his face looked sharper, his blue eyes less brilliant, his forehead creased by lines Malcolm didn't remember.

"That coat needs to dry," Malcolm said. "And I imagine you could do with a seat by the fire."

Oliver took a step forwards and faced him square on, as opponents would before a duel. "I wasn't sure of my welcome."

"You thought I'd throw one of my oldest friends out in the snow?"

"I wasn't sure I qualified as a friend anymore."

Malcolm crossed to the drinks trolley and splashed whisky into two glasses. "We were friends at Oxford. That hasn't changed."

MIDWINTER INTRIGUE

"Even though—"

"I know you were spying on David and Simon and me for Carfax?" The bite of the betrayal and the irony of the parallel to his wife's betrayal bit Malcolm in the throat. He put a glass of whisky in Oliver's hand. "I still saw you as my friend at Oxford. I choose to believe that you saw me as yours."

Oliver's fingers closed round the glass, his knuckles white. "I did. I do."

Malcolm took a swallow of whisky, deeper than he'd intended. "Some things can't be erased, even by Carfax. Especially by Carfax."

Oliver met his gaze. "I'm sorry to arrive unannounced. How's your grandfather?"

"How did you know he was ill?" Malcolm kept his voice even.

"Bel had it from Allie."

That made sense. To preserve the illusion, they wouldn't have been able to let the rest of the family know the reason Strathdon had summoned them to Dunmykel. It didn't mean Carfax didn't know as well. "He's not as ill as we feared," Malcolm said.

"That's a relief." Oliver swallowed. "I'm sure I'm the last person you want to see just now."

"Not quite the last." The words were not entirely filled with irony.

Oliver tossed down a swallow of whisky. "I told him I wasn't the best messenger."

"Carfax sent you."

Oliver grimaced. "Malcolm—"

"I realized he was still watching us in Italy."

"I don't—I've stopped doing errands for him. But he said this could help you and Suzanne. And that for your sakes it wasn't safe to entrust it to anyone else." Oliver's fingers whitened round the glass. "That it might let you come back to Britain."

Malcolm studied his university friend. His parliamentary colleague. His spymaster's agent. "Did he tell you why we left Britain?"

"No. On my honor." Oliver gave a harsh laugh. "Not that I expect you to believe I have any."

"These days I see honor more as an excuse for bad behavior than a guarantee of good." Malcolm would have sworn Oliver was genuinely bewildered as to the reasons for their departure. Of course, Oliver had deceived him about a lot in the past. Malcolm moved to the sofa. "Take

49

your greatcoat off before you catch a chill, Oliver, and then sit down and tell me the whole."

Oliver gave a faint smile that did not reach his eyes, but he shrugged out of the greatcoat and spread it on a bench before the fire, then, after a moment's hesitation, dropped down at the opposite end of the sofa. Malcolm took a sip of whisky. How often had they sat like this, he and Oliver, sharing a drink. Sipping red wine in a coffeehouse or on the floor of their own or their friends' rooms at Oxford. In Berkeley Square or the Lydgates' house in St. James's Place. At Brooks's, strategizing a parliamentary bill before a debate or after a late-night session. "What does Carfax want?"

"He says you have papers. That you'll know the ones I'm talking about. If you share them with him, he'll make it safe for you and Suzanne to return to London."

Malcolm gave a harsh laugh. "Good of him."

"Malcolm." Oliver studied him. "I don't pretend to have the least idea what's going on. I don't pretend to remotely trust Carfax. But I have learned to read him reasonably well. I wouldn't rely on my judgment, but for what it's worth, I think he's sincere."

Malcolm took a sip of whisky. His throat burned. "Carfax couldn't protect us if he wanted to."

Oliver drew a harsh breath, "I know you have no reason to trust me. I'm not sure I'd trust myself with the truth. But if there's anything I can do to help you—"

"Thank you, Oliver." Malcolm was surprised at how free of irony his own voice was. "But as I said, this is beyond even Carfax. We're perfectly happy in Italy."

"You can't pretend this is the life you'd have chosen."

"Are you so content with life in London you can't imagine wanting to leave it?"

Oliver swallowed. "Point taken. But your life isn't mine—"

"I didn't mean—" Malcolm cast a quick glance at his friend. "How's Bel?"

For a moment the pain in Oliver's eyes was as raw as a gaping wound. "She's still living with me, which is probably more than I had any right to expect. She's been spending a lot of time with Mary and the new baby."

"You're away from her and the children at the holidays."

Oliver hunched his shoulders and took a drink of whisky. "In truth, that's part of the reason I agreed to Carfax's request that I come to see you. Bel and the children are at Carfax Court. I couldn't argue with her decision to go. But I also found it hard to stomach time shut up with Carfax. And God knows I don't want the children to see their father and grandfather at odds." Oliver turned his glass in his hand. The firelight bounced off the crystal. "Bel's angry at her father for using me to spy on her brother and his friends. But on balance, she's angrier at me for spying. Or at least in her father's case, her anger is tempered by her concern for her parents. I can't deny what Carfax and Lady Carfax have been through, with Louisa's death and then David leaving the country." He looked up at Malcolm. "That's part of why you left, isn't it? Whyever David and Simon left."

Malcolm met Oliver's gaze steadily. "Surely you realize why David and Simon left."

Oliver returned his gaze. Once, the four of them had confided in each other before anyone else. "Neither of them talked to me before they left. I don't think they talked to much of anyone—they were gone in the middle of the night. But from what I observed, and reading between the lines of the note David left Bel and me, Carfax's pressure on him to marry had become untenable. And David didn't think there was any other way to escape what Carfax might try next."

"I'd say that was a sound judgment."

Oliver continued to watch him. "But what I don't understand is how it connects to you and Suzanne having to leave."

"It doesn't necessarily connect."

Oliver set his glass on the sofa arm with a thud. "I'm a lot of things, Malcolm, but I'm no fool. Somehow all our lives fell apart last June. And in many ways, yours and David's and Simon's more than mine. Certainly I deserved it more. I don't know the connections, but I'm damned sure Carfax is at the heart of all of it." He picked up his glass and took another drink of whisky. "Have you seen David and Simon and the children since they went to the Continent?"

Malcolm shook his head. "They're in France with Simon's relatives and the Sevignys. They were going to come to Italy, but now we're here. We'll see them when we get back." And, despite the careful letters they'd exchanged, Malcolm could not be sure how that meeting would go. For David, so loyal to an ideal of Britain and an ideal of truth, the revelation of Mélanie's spying—and Malcolm's acceptance of it—had been a blow from which Malcolm was not sure their friendship would ever fully recover.

"You're going back to Italy when you leave here, then?" Oliver asked.

"It's our home now. As I said, it's amazing how happy we are there."

Oliver studied him in silence for a moment, the way he might a political opponent whose motives he was trying to decipher. "I can't believe you relish being away from London. I saw you in Parliament. I worked with you in Parliament. I think I know what your work meant to you."

"Frustration?"

"At times. And anger. But it was also a way to fight for what you believed in. To have a stake in shaping the future. It was as though you'd found your true calling."

Memories clustered in his brain. Writing a speech with Mélanie. Strategizing with David and Oliver and Rupert in the Berkeley Square library. Rising to make a speech, hearing his own voice ring out across the House of Commons for the first time. "There are lots of ways to fight, Oliver. And I think my true calling is being father."

Oliver shook his head. "You're a wonderful father, Malcolm. But I don't think you'd limit the scope of your life to that any more than you'd limit Suzanne's to being a mother."

"A palpable hit. But it doesn't change the fact that I'm very fortunate in my life. And that Italy isn't at all a bad place to choose to live it."

Oliver reached inside his coat and drew out a sealed paper. He stared at it a moment, then placed it on the sofa between them, with the care of one handling explosives. "I promised Carfax I'd put this in your hand. Whether or not you read it is entirely up to you."

The handwriting was familiar, going back to boyhood parcels delivered to him and David at Harrow. Malcolm picked it up and slit the seal, as Carfax must have known he would. The contents, of course, were in code. A code Malcolm had devised.

"You'd better stay the night," he told Oliver. "It's going to take me a while to decode this."

"Thank you."

Malcolm got to his feet. "We'd hardly throw you out into the snow." Which was true. It was also true that at this point Malcolm preferred to keep an eye on Oliver.

MIDWINTER INTRIGUE

Oliver pushed himself to his feet. His fingers tightened round his glass. He looked into the fire, then tossed down a swallow of whisky. "Carfax also asked me—" He broke off.

"What?" Malcolm held himself still, watching his university friend. "You're on his side or ours, Oliver. There's no middle ground."

Oliver drew in and released his breath. "He said there might be papers. That your mother had concealed here. Which could affect national security."

"Did you believe him?"

"I wasn't sure what to believe. Carfax wanted me to look for them. He was obviously bargaining on my not telling you."

"Or wanted you to tell me."

Oliver met his gaze. "True. I can never think as far ahead as Carfax."

"Nor can I, most of the time."

"You underrate yourself. Even Carfax admits you can outthink him. But if he wanted me to tell you—Do you think he thinks he can steal whatever it is from you?"

"I don't know."

Mélanie stared at her husband. "Your mother hid something here that Carfax wants?"

"Not to mention the person who broke in two nights ago," Harry added.

"It looks that way. What is anyone's guess." Malcolm cast a glance round the sitting room where they were all gathered. He and Mélanie, Raoul and Laura, Harry and Cordelia, his aunt Frances and her husband Archie. The same group who had helped recover the Elsinore League list in Italy,

"Any idea what it might be?" He addressed this last to Raoul, Archie, and Frances.

Raoul shook his head. "If I'd had the least inkling, I'd have been looking for it myself. But it doesn't surprise me she didn't confide in me."

"If she didn't confide in you, she certainly wouldn't have in me," Archie said.

"I'm not sure," Raoul said. "Sometimes it's easier to confide in someone where there's a bit of distance."

"Perhaps. There were things she told me. But nothing I can connect to anything that might be hidden here."

Frances was frowning. "I arrive here for my great-niece's birthday only to learn that someone has broken into the house looking for something you think my sister hid that may affect national security. I'm used to the unexpected, but this is an adjustment." Her frown deepened. "Arabella told me—I think it was in summer of '98—yes, it must have been, Christopher was starting to walk. I was here to escape the tiresome attentions of Reggie Norquist." She glanced at Archie. "Sorry."

"No need to be," he assured her. "I don't hide my past."

"Arabella came in late one night. That is, she climbed in through my bedchamber window."

"What—" Malcolm said.

His aunt turned to him, her finely plucked brows raised. "My dear Malcolm. Surely at this point you're aware of your mother's activities. Isn't climbing through windows the sort of thing spies do?"

"Yes, but you didn't know about Mama's activities. How on earth did she account—"

Frances regarded him with a gaze that was at once amused and self-contained. "I was never a spy, my dear, but I wasn't precisely a stranger to climbing in and out of windows myself."

Malcolm stared at his aunt. Funny how she and his mother could still surprise him. "Yes, but in her own house—Why would she have felt the need—"

"The house was full of servants. Not to mention your—Alistair."

God, Alistair. "I'm surprised she wasn't worried about running into him in your room," Malcolm said. "Sorry."

"Not in the least. Alistair was occupied elsewhere that night. And I think Arabella was improvising. Her hair was disordered and she was short of breath. I put it down to the obvious explanation, but in retrospect I think I was wrong. She thrust a packet of papers at me and asked me to hide them overnight. On no account to show them to anyone. Particularly Alistair. Then she slipped out into the passage."

"What did you think they were?" Malcolm asked.

"Love letters of some sort." She turned her gaze to Raoul. "Or something you'd given her."

"I wasn't at Dunmykel."

"No, but I knew you were in communication. Your trying to be a husband to Margaret didn't stop you and Arabella from working together."

"True enough," Raoul agreed, his gaze steady on Frances's own. "But not in this case."

"Did you look at the papers?" Malcolm asked.

"I glanced at them," Frances said. "I was too curious not to. They were bound up with buff ribbon with a plain sheet on top. I was sorely tempted to examine the entire packet, but something in Arabella's tone when she'd given me the papers stopped me. That and, I confess, I was quite sure she'd know if I untied them. I tucked them under my mattress. I didn't sleep much that night. The next morning Arabella brought me a cup of chocolate and retrieved the papers. She thanked me profusely and made me swear not to speak of it to anyone. I'd rarely seen her so serious."

"Did she say anything about them again?" Raoul asked.

Frances shook her head. "The next time I saw her was in the drawing room, laughing and flirting with Lord Glenister. Thinking back, knowing what I now know—she must have been desperate indeed to have trusted them to me."

"She was afraid someone was following her and would break into her room," Raoul said. "Perhaps even attack her. The question is where she'd have hidden them after she retrieved them from you."

"The rooms off the secret passage?" Mélanie asked.

"Those were Alistair's," Malcolm said. "Though she might have thought that would have made them a hiding place few could guess at."

Raoul leaned forwards, fingers tented beneath his chin. "She was obviously afraid she was being watched in the house. So it would have to be somewhere she could go without rousing suspicion."

"But not her own rooms," Malcolm said. "She'd have been afraid of those being searched."

"It's so long ago," Frances said. "But I know we were in the drawing room that day. And the Gold Saloon. The dining room, of course, for dinner. Probably the old drawing room."

"The piano?" Certain scenes from Vienna replayed in Mélanie's mind.

"Perhaps," Raoul said. "Though I'd think she'd have been worried someone would think of it."

"She could have tucked it into a book and moved it later," Archie said. "I'd have been here, though I can't swear to remembering the exact day. Arabella read, but she didn't spend a great deal of time in the library at social gatherings. But there were always books about the other rooms.

If she'd had time later, she could have hollowed something out or created a better hiding place."

"She wouldn't have wanted to touch the papers for a while, though," Raoul said. "If she took them from someone who was at the house party or suspected others at Dunmykel were after them."

"So it's something to do with the Elsinore League?" Cordelia asked.

"That's the obvious explanation," Archie said. "Though it doesn't explain why Carfax is suddenly looking for the papers now."

"Not to mention whoever broke in," Mélanie said. "Unless that person is working for Carfax too."

"Could she have stolen them from Alistair?" Malcolm asked Frances. "Or been hiding them from him?"

"Perhaps both," Frances said. "Though it makes one wonder why she chose to give them to me."

"It sounds as though she didn't have a lot of choice," Malcolm said. Much as he now knew about her past, he was still getting used to the image of his mother scaling the walls of Dunmykel.

"Besides, she knew you were her sister," Raoul said.

"My dear Raoul," Frances said, turning to her friend, "if you had the least idea of what sisters can do to each other—"

"Some sisters. Bella knew what you valued underneath."

Frances tucked a curl behind her ear. "You're talking sentimental twaddle again. It must be impending fatherhood."

Raoul reached across from his chair to the settee where Frances was sitting with Archie and flicked a finger against her cheek. "Touché, Fanny."

"'98," Archie said. "The time of the Uprising."

"Quite." Raoul's mobile face went serious. "One could well imagine information being vital then. Harder to see why it's of such moment now."

"If they could use it against someone," Harry said.

Malcolm nodded. "After all, O'Roarke, the League want you dead."

"You think Bella hid information that could damage Raoul?" Frances said. "You'd think she'd have destroyed it."

"Unless it was valuable for other reasons." Malcolm held his father's gaze across the room. "Well?"

"What other secrets did I have in '98? A lot, at the time. I knew where Edward Fitzgerald was and a host of others. I knew—I'd devised—the codes we were using to communicate. I knew where weapons were stashed. But it's hard to see why any of that would be worth all this fuss now. Hard, in fact, to see why Bella wouldn't have destroyed it at the time. Unless she was thinking of trading it for something else."

Malcolm could not quite control his indrawn gasp. "Information is currency," Raoul said. "Arabella and I were allied in most things. But not always."

"Did Carfax send Oliver here just to search for whatever this is?" Cordelia asked. "He seems an unlikely choice for a searcher."

"No," Malcolm said. "That's not the only reason." He drew out his decoded version of Carfax's letter. "You should all see this."

Chapter 8

*M*y *dear Malcolm,*

One of your many strengths has always been your ability to see your own prejudices. Often to a fault. But I beg in this case you will look past the anger I have no doubt you are feeling with me. I won't insult us both by pretending we don't have our differences. But we both recognize the threat posed by the Elsinore League. I know you have the list of League members. Even you must admit that I have connections and knowledge that could be helpful in putting that list to use.

As you'll know, Mélanie's history has not become common knowledge. If you come back to Britain, you won't be in any greater danger than you were in before. I can help keep Mélanie's secrets. I can help you escape back to Italy should the unexpected happen. I won't ask you to accept my word, but if you feel you need a guarantee of my good behavior, you can share the list a few names at a time.

Work with me on this. Our differing philosophies aside, I think you'll acknowledge we've always worked together well. Nothing that's passed between us has changed my estimation of your abilities, and I flatter myself you must still have some respect for mine. We may have different visions of what we want for Britain, but the Elsinore League pose a threat to both. I'd welcome Mélanie's talents as well. I always had a great deal of respect for her, and the revelations about her past demonstrate just how formidable she is.

Italy is a beautiful country, but you're wasted there. You certainly made a stir in Parliament, little as I agreed with you. I assume you want to get back to making outrageous speeches and proposing legislation that will never come to pass. I beg you, Malcolm, don't let your prejudices stand in the way. Do what's best for your family and your country and come back.

MIDWINTER INTRIGUE

Yours, etc....
Carfax

P.S. Oh, you're probably wondering about O'Roarke. I assume guaranteeing his safety as well is part of any alliance you'll form with me. Besides, much as it may pain me to admit it, we could use his talents as well.

Malcolm stared at the decoded version of Carfax's letter against the faded red and gold tapestry of a footstool where Harry had placed it when they were finished passing it round.

"We should have seen this coming," Archie said.

"Probably," Malcolm agreed. "I'm sharing it because you're all involved in this investigation one way and another. But I think it's quite obvious what the answer has to be. One could argue I was mad to work with Carfax the first time. I'm hardly insane enough to do so again."

Mélanie was staring at the letter, brows drawn, arms folded across her chest. "Darling—"

Malcolm spun towards his wife. "You can't be suggesting we trust Carfax, of all people."

"I can't imagine ever trusting Carfax. But he said six months ago he wouldn't expose my past himself—"

"And you believed—"

"No, but I don't think he'd do it without reason. And right now, it's in his self-interest to protect all of us. He needs our help."

"And when he stops needing it?"

"He says it himself. We'd be in no greater danger than before."

"But we didn't know the danger we were in before." Malcolm scraped a hand through his hair. "I still grow cold when I realize the risks we ran all those years."

"We're always going to run risks, darling."

Malcolm dropped down on the dressing table bench beside his wife and seized her hands. "This isn't just Carfax. God knows who else in Britain knows about you. Including members of the League."

"Which makes it all the more important to checkmate them."

Harry was looking from Raoul to Archie. "Could Carfax help with the list?"

Raoul and Archie exchanged a long look, heavy with the weight of all their years working together against the League.

59

"Possibly," Archie said. "He has leverage we don't. And for all I've been a League member myself for years, he may have information about them we don't."

"We still don't know what secrets he got when he traded intelligence with Fouché for information about the League eight years ago," Raoul said. "But sharing information also poses risks—"

"Christ, Raoul," Malcolm said. "I can't believe you're even considering—"

"I always try to consider every option, Malcolm. I thought I'd taught you to do the same."

Malcolm drew a breath. "Point taken."

"As I was saying," Raoul continued, "once Carfax has the intelligence, we don't know what he may do with it. We now have Sanderson reporting to us. I wouldn't lightly expose any asset to Carfax, even an asset in the League. On the other hand, we could try to keep Sanderson out of it."

Archie nodded. The list of Elsinore League names they had recovered in Italy in September had ultimately given them the leverage to persuade Roger Sanderson to work with them. It hadn't given them the break they needed against the League yet, but it was a start. "We certainly wouldn't share the whole list. But we could use a few names to draw Carfax out. See what he has to share himself."

Frances frowned. "That sounds like playing with fire."

Archie reached for his wife's hand. "What do you think we've been doing for the past twenty years, my darling?"

"Archie and I could talk to Carfax," Raoul said. "There'd be no need for anyone else to leave Scotland."

Malcolm shot a look at his father. "You may be more at risk than any of us. The Elsinore League still want you dead."

"They haven't tried anything in months," Raoul said.

"There was that skirmish that nearly took your eye out." Laura reached up to touch the scar beside his right eye.

"That would have been a very roundabout way for them to try to kill someone." Raoul caught her hand and pressed it to his lips.

"The Elsinore League have been known to be roundabout. They've been known to be just about anything in pursuit of their enemies," Laura said.

"Possibly," Raoul admitted. "But we have no proof they were behind it."

MIDWINTER INTRIGUE

"You aren't going anywhere near the Elsinore League or Carfax or any of the British authorities with your child about to be born in less than six months, O'Roarke," Malcolm said.

Rather to his surprise, Raoul went quiet.

"I've still got the regent's ear enough to offer me protection," Archie said. "I could talk to Carfax."

"Yes, we certainly can't all hide forever." Frances smoothed the lavender twilled sarcenet of her skirt over her expanding stomach. "Babies or not."

Archie frowned. "For a number of reasons, I think it might be best if you remained in Scotland."

"Archie, don't you dare," Frances said. "You promised not to wrap me in cotton wool."

"And you promised not to run unnecessary risks."

"It's not in the least unnecessary. I don't deny your influence with the regent, but it's nothing compared to mine."

Archie smiled. "I can't argue with that. It doesn't stop me from worrying."

"Which still doesn't mean we should be sharing any of this with Carfax, risk or not." Malcolm leaned forwards and swung his gaze round the company. "We have Sanderson. We're gaining intelligence. Putting my feelings about Carfax out of it—which I confess is difficult to do—I think it's too great a risk to share anything with Carfax. We can't control his agenda. We can't be sure he wouldn't decide to make an alliance with the League instead of trying to bring them down."

"Hasn't he been fighting them for years?" Cordelia said. "He was willing to trade information to Fouché to combat them."

"Which proves how very flexible Carfax is in his alliances," Malcolm said. "You can't imagine the League wouldn't try to co-opt him. Or that Carfax wouldn't try to use information about the League to blackmail them for his own ends. Even if he did follow through and succeed in destroying them, I grow cold at the thought of the League's blackmail information falling into Carfax's hands."

Raoul inclined his head. "I won't argue with that."

"Nor will I," Archie said. "But I still wonder if we shouldn't pretend to negotiate. Try to draw him out."

"It's an option," Malcolm said. "But not one I'm prepared to pursue yet."

Mélanie pushed the door of their bedchamber to and leaned against the panels. "I'm sorry, darling."

"For what?" Malcolm asked.

"We were hardly in agreement just now."

"Good God, Mel, I'd never expect us to agree about everything. I'd be rather horrified if we did. And that was before I knew we'd fought on opposite sides for close to a decade." He studied her for a moment. "Though I can't believe you, of all people, were suggesting we work with Carfax."

"I don't know. I've always been more pragmatic about the alliances I'll form than you."

"Hardly. I worked against my principles for almost a decade. I'm not doing so again."

"Malcolm." Mélanie stared at her husband, shocked at the bitterness in his tone. "No one could blame you for working for your country."

"No? You can't honestly tell me you'd work for France right now."

"Of course not, but—"

Malcolm held her gaze, his own a surprising wasteland. "Point taken, I think."

"Darling." Mélanie went up to him and slid her arms round him. "You didn't know the man Carfax was when you went to work for him."

"Didn't I? I'd grown up with him."

"He'd hardly have shown the man he was to you as a boy."

"I was out of Oxford by the time I went to work for him. I may not have known the tactics he was capable of, but I knew what he stood for. I knew it was opposed to just about everything I stood for. And I still went to work for him."

"You needed a purpose. And after what you'd been through—"

"I hadn't been through what you'd been through." Malcolm smoothed a strand of hair off her temple. "And you found a purpose that didn't make a mockery of your ideals."

Mélanie stared up at her husband. "How long have you been thinking this way?"

"I've had qualms about working for Carfax for years. You know that. But those qualms could hardly fail to have increased after his actions last June. And in Italy I had leisure to reflect on what he'd done. On what I've done through the years."

"Malcolm. Dearest. You're the best person I know. I can't bear to think of you blaming yourself."

He gave a wintry smile. "You've warned me not to idealize you, sweetheart. Don't you think the same is true of me?" He tucked a curl behind her ear. "Don't let your own guilt make you see me as something other than what I am. I'm a passably good agent who's managed to hold on to some shreds of conscience. But I'm also a man who sold out his ideals and did the errands of men I violently disagreed with. Hardly the stuff to idealize."

"Darling." She took his face between her hands. "If I have any understanding of love or goodness, it's only because I got it from you."

"And if I have a shred of ability to put my ideals into practice, it's only because I got it from you."

"You were very young when you went to work for Carfax."

"Not as young as you were when you went to work for O'Roarke."

"But you hadn't been through what I had. Not that you hadn't been through a lot, but—I don't know that you knew what the war was about."

"And when I learned? Long before I met you. How long did it take me to leave? It must have driven you mad in Lisbon and Vienna and Brussels and Paris, watching me do the bidding of people you despised. People I despised."

Mélanie pressed her hands against his chest. "But that's just it, darling. You didn't despise Carfax. Or Wellington or Castlereagh. You put your loyalty to them first. You've always been loyal to people. Whereas I found a purpose I thought was worth more than any sort of personal loyalty."

Malcolm's hands closed over her own. "It's not that simple, sweetheart. I may be loyal to people, but it doesn't mean there aren't things I believe in. And I've seen just how loyal you and Raoul are to your comrades and the people you love."

"Now who's idealizing, Malcolm?"

"For God's sake, Mel. Raoul did his best to pull a smoke screen over his actions for years, but we both know better now. In truth, I can't believe he deceived us so well for so long. I know what you and Raoul risked for Manon. For Lisette. For Queen Hortense. For Josephine. For a score of others. What Raoul's done for us. What you did for Marthe and others. Don't pretend otherwise."

"I wouldn't. But you can't deny he and I both made compromises."

"Of course. Every agent does. What I'm also saying is in some ways those compromises are nothing beside the ones I've made."

"Malcolm—"

"Because I betrayed myself."

"You stopped, Malcolm. You left off being an agent, as much as anyone can."

His fingers tightened over her own. "So did you, my darling. Years before I did."

Mélanie stared at him. "I didn't—"

"You compromised yourself much less than I did. But you found it intolerable long before I did."

"I never—"

She broke off as a rap fell on the door. "I'm sorry." Gisèle slipped into the room. "But Grandfather asked me to fetch you. Insisted on it, actually. We've caught sight of a boat approaching. He says it's his plan."

Chapter 9

The moonlight sparked off the diamond head of a walking stick as the boatman handed a man ashore, followed by a cloaked woman. The man moved into the light, but even before he did, Malcolm knew.

"Prince Talleyrand," he said, going forwards to greet the statesman. "I wondered if it was you. But I wasn't sure Grandfather would actually summon you."

Talleyrand gave an amused smile. "I think you underestimate how seriously we all take your predicament, my boy."

"Doro." Malcolm leaned forwards to kiss Dorothée de Talleyrand-Périgord's cheek.

Dorothée squeezed his arm. "It's good to see you, Malcolm." She held out her hands to Mélanie. "Suzanne. Mélanie. *Chérie.*"

Mélanie ran forwards to hug her friend. Malcolm saw the way her arms closed tight round Dorothée. He could guess what it meant to Mel to see a friend in the midst of everything. He couldn't deny he was glad to see them both himself. And yet, despite the fact that he had been half expecting it, Talleyrand's arrival was a damnable complication.

Talleyrand took a sip of calvados. "Stop looking at me as though I'm going to bite, Malcolm. I'm on your side. This time." He settled back in his chair in the room Gisèle had shown him to. "I trust we can now dispense with the pretense that anyone doesn't know anything. I don't deny Carfax's power. I've been bested by him in the past. But surely you realize that in the past three decades I've amassed information I can use against him."

"I don't doubt it," Malcolm said. "Just as I don't doubt he has information he could use against you."

Talleyrand lifted a brow. "You think I haven't considered that?"

The prince was a master at playing the chess game of diplomatic and political intrigue without putting himself in check. Malcolm had to acknowledge that. He would trust Talleyrand with a lot. But this was the safety of his family.

"I've had dealings with Carfax," Talleyrand said.

"Yes, I know," Malcolm returned, not trying to keep the dryness from his voice. During the Napoleonic Wars, Talleyrand, out of power, had made overtures to the British. He'd even sent one of his agents to work with them in the Peninsula. An agent who happened to be Malcolm's illegitimate half-sister.

"I'll approach him myself," Talleyrand said. "I'll make the consequences clear should any harm befall Mélanie."

Malcolm stared at the prince. The man he'd known since he was a boy of five. The man with whom he'd crossed diplomatic swords in Vienna. "It's a very generous offer."

"I'm not in Carfax's reach the way people in Britain are."

"Still—"

"I could say it's a debt I owe your mother, which would be true." Talleyrand glanced at Strathdon, who was observing the scene with quiet command. "But the truth is I also owe a great deal to you. And to Mélanie and O'Roarke." Talleyrand nodded at Mélanie and Raoul. "And I confess it would be quite satisfying to strike a blow at Britain's spymaster. Call it getting a bit of my own back."

"I understand the impulse," Malcolm said. "But Carfax isn't the only one in Britain who knows about Mélanie. He himself admitted he couldn't control the information. And we don't know whom else he may have told."

"He also wanted you out of Britain and away from David," Mélanie said.

"All the more reason for him to have told more people so we can't go back."

"Carfax is a lot of things, but he's no fool," Talleyrand said. "He doesn't slam a door shut unless he has to. He wouldn't want to make it impossible for you to return to Britain. Not out of the goodness of his heart, but because he'd want the option of seeking your services in the future."

"It's a good point," Raoul said.

"Possibly," Malcolm acknowledged. "But even without Carfax, an intolerable number of the Elsinore League know."

"And they also won't use the information lightly." Talleyrand stretched out his clubfoot.

"No, they'll use it to try to force Mélanie to do their bidding. They already have."

"And she's avoided doing so." Talleyrand took another sip of calvados. "My dear boy, you can always leave again."

"You must see the risk." Malcolm cast a glance towards the adjoining room where Dorothée had gone to unpack. "I don't think you're a stranger to understanding family feeling."

"Perhaps not. But I also understand the value of taking risks." Talleyrand set down his glass. "Think about it. Neither Doro nor I has any intention of turning about and leaving immediately, not in this weather with the holidays approaching."

"We wouldn't dream of letting you leave without a proper visit," Strathdon said. "Plenty of time to debate the details further."

"Of course we're delighted to have you here." Malcolm started to push himself to his feet, then said, "There's one more thing, sir. Someone broke into the house two nights ago searching for something Arabella hid here in 1798. Carfax appears to be after it as well. Do you have any idea what it might be?"

Talleyrand's brows lifted in rare surprise. "When did this start?"

"Just now, so far as we know. So it's something that's suddenly relevant now, or that those seeking it have just learned about."

The prince shook his head. "I can imagine any number of things your mother might have had of interest to Carfax. Or others. But I know of nothing specific. By '98 I had returned to France."

"You were still in close communication with my mother. You set her after the Elsinore League."

Talleyrand's gaze locked on Malcolm's across the room. This was the first time the two had met since Malcolm had learned of his mother's quest to bring down the League, and of Talleyrand's role, which was still partly supposition. "I wouldn't say I set her after them. She'd already heard rumors. I confirmed what I knew, and gave her what other information I could. At the time, after her unfortunate entanglement with Peter of Courland, and Tatiana's birth, she badly needed distraction." Talleyrand reached for his glass. "I may also have thought it would be useful to discover more about the League."

"She must have updated you about what she learned."

"At times. I doubt she told me everything. I doubt she told anyone everything. Including O'Roarke."

"Very much including me," Raoul said.

"You look well." Mélanie smiled at Dorothée across the bedchamber Gisèle had allotted to Doro, seemingly unfazed by the last-minute guests. Malcolm's little sister had become an accomplished hostess.

"Thank you." Doro looked up from taking her toiletries from her velvet-lined mahogany dressing case. She was—quite uncharacteristically for her—traveling without a maid. "I don't deny I miss being at the heart of things. But I find our life is"—Dorothée colored, almost like the schoolgirl she had been not so very long ago—"surprisingly agreeable."

"How are the boys?"

"Thriving. Clattering about the house. Talleyrand says they keep him young." Doro's gaze flickered over Mélanie's face. "You look well, as well. I know the past months can't have been easy."

Mélanie plucked at the rose-striped lustring of her gown. "Italy is also surprisingly agreeable. I can't forget what Malcolm has lost, and I'm sure he can't either, but we've neither of us gone mad with boredom as I'd feared. I don't think he looks at me and hates me for what he's lost."

"Dearest." Doro went still, silver-backed brush in one hand. "I'm sure he could never hate you."

"Even now you know the truth about me?"

Dorothée regarded her without flinching. "Perhaps especially now. I've seen the way he looks at you. Still."

Mélanie perched on the edge of the bed. "I think—I know—he loves me." Funny to be able to say that. "But—what was it you were saying about not being at the heart of things? We both miss that. Even if part of being at the heart of things is Almack's and the Queen's Drawing Rooms. At the same time, in some ways I've never been more free. Not to have to pretend. Not to dress for dinner unless one wants to. Not to feel pulled away from the children."

Doro set the brush down beside her comb and mirror. "But you still want to go back?"

Mélanie hugged her arms over the blonde lace frill on her bodice. "I'd give almost anything to give Malcolm back what he's lost because of me. Though I don't think either of us wants to go back to precisely the life we had before. Practically, I don't think we could."

Dorothée took a black velvet jewelry pouch from the dressing case. "Lady Tarrington would go back with you. I understand she's expecting Mr. O'Roarke's child."

"We couldn't leave her. We wouldn't want to. The children adore her, and her daughter. They're part of our family."

"As is Mr. O'Roarke."

Mélanie drew a breath. A year ago, when Malcolm had learned the truth of her past, she hadn't thought their marriage could survive as anything more than a façade for the sake of the children. If anyone had told her that Malcolm would view Raoul as his father, and they'd all be part of the same household—"It seems mad," she said. "But somehow we're a family."

Dorothée turned, leaning against the dressing table. "I live with my husband's uncle. Who used to be my mother's lover. I'm hardly one to cast aspersions. Or to fail to applaud any arrangement that makes people happy."

Mélanie met her friend's gaze. Her mind went back to those days in Vienna. She'd been unsure of Malcolm's feelings, tormented by her fear that he loved another woman. Doro had been trembling on the brink of an affair with Karl Clam-Martinitz, yet at the same time, half in love with Talleyrand, though she couldn't quite put it into words yet. They'd made confidences to each other they'd made to few others. And all the while, Mélanie had been spying for the Bonapartists. "Doro—It must have been a shock to learn the truth." She'd had the luxury of telling most of her friends. Doro would have learned from Talleyrand, countries away from her.

"That you were spying for the Bonapartists?" Dorothée gave an unexpected laugh. "*Chérie*, given the number of times Talleyrand has changed his allegiance—officially and unofficially—do you really think I'd cast aspersions over that either?"

"But you might over the fact that I was lying to you."

"Were you?" Doro tilted her head to one side, her brown ringlets swinging beside her face. "It's true you didn't tell me the full truth of who you were. But, which of us does? I don't think you were lying when you listened to my uncertainty over my feelings for Karl or my grief over my poor little girl or my confusion about my uncle. At least, not unless you're a very good liar indeed."

"No. Of course not. But—"

Dorothée crossed the room and dropped down on the embroidered satin coverlet beside Mélanie. "I don't think you were lying about your feelings for Malcolm or your worries about Princess Tatiana or your love for Colin. I'm quite sure all those were real."

"Yes, but—"

"So, I did know the real you."

"In some ways." Mélanie gripped her hands together. In those days she hadn't been sure *she'd* known the real her. Sometimes she still wasn't sure she did. "Just not all of me."

"Which of us knows all of anyone? Even those whose bed we share. Even those we pledge our lives to. Officially or unofficially." Dorothée put her hand over Mélanie's. "I grew up in a world of secrets and deceptions. Yours bothers me less than most."

Mélanie squeezed her friend's hand. "It's good to see you again."

"You too. And at least we'll have some time. With the weather, we won't be able to leave right away. And Talleyrand isn't going to give up on convincing Malcolm of his plan. We'll be able to keep Christmas with you."

"And I couldn't be happier about it. But you'll be away from the boys."

Doro's brows drew together. "It won't be the first time. Or the last, I suspect. One grows used to separations with the lives we lead. I've never been able to take them everywhere with me as you do with yours. And I have far more time with them now than I did when Talleyrand was in power and our life was a whirlwind. One makes the most of the circumstances in which one finds oneself. Isn't that the lesson we learned in Vienna?"

"I quite like it." From the half-landing, baby Ian on her hip, Gisèle surveyed the towering fir tree four footmen had set up in the great hall under Dorothée's supervision.

"Wait until we add ribbon," Dorothée said. "And candles, though probably not until Christmas Eve."

"I remember the one in Vienna." Colin was leaning over the stair rail with Emily, Livia, and Chloe. The four of them had avidly watched the tree go up. "We had one at home last year, but it wasn't as big."

Mélanie, holding Jessica up where she could see the tree without grabbing, smiled at the excitement in her son's voice, though she swallowed a pang at the easy way he referred to Berkeley Square as home. She had put a smaller tree up in the Berkeley Square drawing room last year, determined to wring enjoyment out of the holidays as she and Malcolm adjusted to the fragile rapprochement that was their marriage. But this was the first time the German tradition had come to Dunmykel.

"In Vienna at the Congress, they called it 'Christmas à la Berlin,'" Dorothée said, stepping back to admire the tree. "I'm glad we've brought it to Scotland."

"Need gold," Drusilla said, wriggling in Cordy's arms.

"Quite right," Cordelia agreed. "Wait until we have it decorated."

"What do you put on top?" A rat-a-tat that sounded like gunfire cut the air of the hall. Mélanie realized it was Emily's shoes tapping on the wood of the stairs as she bounced up and down in excitement.

"A star, I think." Laura moved down the stairs to stand behind her daughter. "At least, that's what we used at ho—in Berkeley Square."

"I have a lovely set of gold and crystal ones in Paris," Dorothée said, looking up at the children. "But we can make one out of gold paper. You can help me, Emily."

Emily grinned at Doro, entranced. Dorothée might be practically royalty, but she had always had the ability to disarm children. Mélanie remembered her entrancing Colin when he was younger than Jessica was now. How long ago the Congress seemed. And yet, in some ways, it was as though it had been yesterday.

"An admirable tradition," Lady Frances said. "I can't think why we haven't adopted it. But then, as with porcelain stoves, there are so many sensible customs on the Continent we've been slow to adopt in Britain."

Gisèle glanced at the footmen, who were leaning against the paneling. Even with four of them it had been an exhausting task to get the tree in. "Time for a break for everyone, I think, while we strategize what to do next."

Between the search for Arabella Rannoch's hidden secrets (which so far had produced no results) and the holiday decorating (which was a welcome distraction for snowbound children and adults alike), it had been an exhausting week for the Dunmykel staff, though Mélanie consoled herself with the recollection that the gleam in their eyes suggested they welcomed the excitement.

The ladies and children adjourned to the old drawing room, a favorite room of Arabella's, dominated by her Broadwood grand

71

pianoforte (the piano and room had been pulled apart by both servants and family to no avail in the search for the papers). It was less formal than other rooms in the house, the canvaswork furniture and Savonnerie carpet slightly faded. In this room, Mélanie found the thought of her mother-in-law less intimidating. If Arabella could have been comfortable here, Mélanie could almost imagine relaxing with her over a cup of tea. Or a glass of wine.

The footmen brought in both, as well as cakes and sandwiches, and lemonade for the children. Gisèle thanked them, and Mélanie added that she hoped they could enjoy some quiet, as surely the house would settle down. Oliver had managed to depart the morning after his arrival, saying he might be able to be at Carfax Court in time for Christmas, but it was not as though, the snow still falling, there was a great need to stay alert for callers. But Mélanie was just settling into the chintz window seat cushions, Jessica in her lap and a glass of claret between her fingers, when Alec returned, his livery coat back on. He went to Gisèle and bent to whisper in her ear. Gisèle listened, put Ian in Lady Frances's arms, cast a quick "I'll deal with this" look at Mélanie, and got to her feet. Mélanie remained where she was. After all, whoever might technically own Dunmykel, practically it was much more Gisèle and Andrew's than her own and Malcolm's. She was essentially a guest.

But a quarter hour later, Alec returned and bent this time to whisper in Mélanie's ear. "I'm sorry, madam. But Mrs. Thirle asks if you can come down to the library. I've summoned Mr. Rannoch as well."

Malcolm met his wife's gaze as she descended the stairs. He'd been in the midst of going through the papers in his mother's escritoire for the tenth time when Alec brought him Gisèle's message. "Do you know—?" he asked.

Mélanie shook her head. "Alec came in to fetch Gisèle, and then a quarter hour later Gelly asked me to join her."

Malcolm pulled open the library door and followed his wife into the room to see two people standing before the fireplace. A familiar white-blond head was bent close to his sister's red-blonde ringlets. Malcolm pushed the door to, disbelief ringing in his head.

Gisèle turned round with a quick smile at the click of the door closing. "Look who's come in out of the snow."

MIDWINTER INTRIGUE

"Rannoch, Suzanne." Tommy Belmont crossed to Malcolm and Mélanie with one of his quick, easy smiles. "As I was telling Miss Fraser—Mrs. Thirle, that is—I was on my way to my father's hunting box when the weather took a turn for the worse, and I realized I was within an hour of Dunmykel. I hope you'll forgive the invasion."

"I forgot your father had a box in Scotland," Malcolm said. "And of course you're welcome, as I'm sure Gisèle told you."

"Tommy." Mélanie held out her hand. Tommy bowed over it and lifted it to his lips.

Gallantry had always been more in Tommy's line than Malcolm's, for all Belmont was an avowed cynic about romantic relationships. Like Malcolm, Tommy Belmont had been a diplomatic attaché and they had served together in Lisbon and at the Congress of Vienna. And, like Malcolm, Tommy had also been an agent for Carfax. Malcolm would be sure Carfax had sent him now, were it not that Carfax had already sent Oliver. But Malcolm didn't for a moment believe Belmont had simply happened upon Dunmykel due to a convenient storm.

Gisèle gave a bright smile. She'd always liked Tommy, and seemed uncharacteristically blind to the undercurrents between him and Malcolm. "I'll arrange for your room, Mr. Belmont."

Tommy watched the door close behind her. "Hard to believe she's married and a mother. One forgets how time passes."

"Nothing like having children to bring that home." Mélanie moved to the sofa. Her smile was disarming, but Malcolm had no doubt she had as many questions about Tommy's arrival as he did himself.

"Yes, I forget, given the lives you lead, how domestic you are. Though I understand you've been living quietly in Italy."

"We're very happy there." Malcolm crossed to the drinks trolley and splashed whisky into three glasses. "Why are you here, Belmont?"

"So sure I have an ulterior purpose?"

"Do you really have to ask that?" Malcolm put one of the whiskies into Mélanie's hand and held out a second to Tommy.

Tommy reached out to take the drink, but as he stretched out his hand, his legs buckled under him. The glass tumbled from his fingers and thudded to the floor, spattering whisky. Tommy collapsed in a heap on the Aubusson carpet.

73

Chapter 10

Malcolm dropped to the carpet. Mélanie had already sprung from the sofa and was unbuttoning Tommy's coat. A spreading crimson stain showed against his blue silk waistcoat.

"Stupid," Tommy muttered. "Thought I had it bandaged."

"Don't try to talk, Tommy." Mélanie was unbuttoning Tommy's waistcoat. "Malcolm, get my medical box."

"Always thought it would be pleasant to have you undress me," Tommy muttered between hoarse breaths. "But this isn't what I had in mind."

"Don't waste your breath on fantasies, Tommy." Mélanie pushed Tommy's waistcoat back and tugged his shirt from his breeches. He or someone else had bound a makeshift bandage that appeared to be made of a cravat round his chest. She unknotted the ends and peeled it back. Despite her care, Tommy sucked in his breath. The wound was long and jagged and crisscrossed his chest. It had been crudely stitched, but the stitches had broken open, probably when he dismounted and came into the house, and it was bleeding freely. She pressed a clean fold of the bandage over it until Malcolm returned with her medical box.

"How bad is it?" he asked, dropping down beside her again.

"Hard to tell. It looks to have missed his heart and lungs. He needs stitches, and we have to get the bleeding stopped. I'm going to need you to hold him still."

She cleaned the wound with whisky. The pressure had stopped the bleeding enough that she was able to redo the stitches. Malcolm kept his hands on Tommy's shoulders, but Tommy mercifully appeared to have fainted again.

"Will he live?" Malcolm asked in an even voice.

Mélanie cast a quick glance up at her husband. He looked more concerned than one might have expected, given his professed opinion of

Tommy Belmont. "He will if we can hold off wound fever," she said. "But it looks as if we have another long-term guest."

"Someone attacked Tommy Belmont?" Cordelia said.

"That's undeniable, judging by his wound," Mélanie said. They had gathered in her and Malcolm's bedchamber to update the two Davenport couples and Laura and Raoul on Tommy's sudden arrival. "And, talking of coincidence, I don't think it was highwaymen."

"Someone who didn't want him to get here?" Harry suggested. "If he's bringing another offer from Carfax—the Elsinore League?"

"Possible," Malcolm said. "Usually they're more efficient in their work. But then they don't usually go up against men like Belmont."

"Or someone who wants something from Tommy," Mélanie suggested.

"Whatever this thing is that people think is hidden at Dunmykel," Cordelia said, "could Carfax have sent Tommy after it? Or could someone think Tommy already has it?"

"Possibly," Malcolm said. "And I'd say it's very likely Carfax sent Tommy after it, since he sent Oliver. Perhaps that's why he sent both of them to Dunmykel. But until Tommy recovers, we can only speculate."

Tommy's face was as pale as the Irish linen of the pillowcase, but his eyes were clear and focused. It had been touch and go for a day or two, but Mélanie now assured Malcolm he should make a full recovery. "Suzanne's wasted on civilian life," Tommy said. "For a number of reasons. So are you, if it comes to that, though I can't say I miss your annoying scruples. Help me sit up, Rannoch, there's a good fellow."

Malcolm slid a pillow behind Tommy's shoulders. "It's good to see you've got your tongue back, Belmont."

"You really thought I was done for, didn't you? You wouldn't be so conciliatory otherwise." Tommy settled back against the pillow. "Where were we when I so ingloriously fainted?"

"I was asking what the devil you were doing here."

"You jump at shadows, Rannoch."

75

"I know you, Belmont. Very little you do isn't carefully calculated. Did you really think I'd believe that farrago about losing your way in the storm?"

Tommy examined his nails. "People lose their way in storms."

"People do. You don't."

Tommy caught and held Malcolm's gaze with his own. "You can't expect me to believe you're happy in Italy."

For a moment, the echo of the children's shouts off the tile on the villa terrace sounded in Malcolm's mind. He could taste the sweet bite of chilled wine on a warm afternoon. "In many ways," he said, "there are few places I've been happier."

Tommy's brows drew together, as though Malcolm had gone off-script. "You can't tell me you don't miss—"

"I think one misses things from parts of one's old life everywhere. I even miss things from Lisbon. I even miss you at times."

"My God, Rannoch. The Italian sun has addled your brain." Tommy's gaze shifted over Malcolm's face. "You can't tell me you wouldn't like to come back."

"To Brooks's and Almack's and fog and soot?"

"To sea air and friends and being able to speak your mind in Parliament. To the dream of a Britain I've never quite been able to see but can glimpse enough to know that you do." Tommy tilted his head back. "It could happen, you know. You could be safe. Suzanne could be safe."

Malcolm willed himself to relax back in his chair. "Good of you, Tommy, but I see no reason why my wife shouldn't be safe."

"Let's dispense with the fencing, Rannoch. I can make you guarantees. You'd be wise to listen before you decide to remain in exile."

"My God." Malcolm pushed himself to his feet. "Carfax did send you. He thought Oliver wouldn't be persuasive enough? Carfax is a lot of things, but he's not usually wasteful. He sent his son-in-law here at Christmas—"

Tommy let out a whoop of laughter. "Malcolm, no. Though I suppose I should have realized you'd think of that."

"Given that you work for Carfax, it's not a difficult deduction."

"You, of all people, should realize that isn't an unchangeable relationship."

Malcolm stared at his colleague. His former colleague. "Whom are you working for?"

MIDWINTER INTRIGUE

A lazy grin spread across Tommy's face. The sort of grin that had been maddening Malcolm from the day he arrived in Lisbon as an attaché. "I was sure you'd have that worked out by now."

Malcolm's gaze locked on Tommy's own. He'd never precisely have called Belmont a friend. But they'd strategized missions together. Sat up late writing dispatches over endless pots of coffee. Endured the grinding monotony of diplomatic receptions, where sometimes a mumbled off-color joke was the only way to stave off boredom, and the risks behind French lines. On at least one occasion, he was quite sure he owed Tommy his life. "You're working for the Elsinore League."

"Knew you'd work it out. Pour me a glass of brandy, there's a good fellow."

"Tommy—"

"I know your tiresome scruples, but you should equally know I haven't any scruples at all. Besides, we both know we violated every shred of anything that could be called honor working for Carfax. Do I have to ask for the brandy again? I'm actually rather uncomfortable."

Which from Tommy meant he was in a good deal of pain. Malcolm moved to the table by the windows that held a decanter and poured a finger of brandy into a glass. In many ways, Tommy would have been a prime candidate for the League. The third son of an earl, well off and with impeccable bloodlines, but without property or position to occupy him. Too much of a cynic to find fulfillment or ties in love or starting a family of his own, at least so far. And in all their years abroad, he'd never seemed to particularly miss his parents or siblings, though he wasn't estranged from them. And yet—

Malcolm crossed back to the bed and put the glass in Tommy's hand. "Your father isn't a League member."

"So sure that list you have is complete?" Tommy took a grateful sip of brandy. "Oh, yes, I know about the list. I don't think it is complete. And I don't know if you'll believe me, but as it happens my father isn't a League member. But my godfather is. Lord Beverston. Always took rather a kind interest in me."

Malcolm dropped back into his chair. Beverston was a senior League member. One of the founders, along with Alistair. "I forgot Beverston was your godfather. He also recruited his son into the League." Malcolm had crossed paths with Beverston's son, John Smythe, in their recent adventure in Italy.

"Yes, I know." Tommy regarded Malcolm for a moment. "You didn't kill him, did you?"

77

"No, as it happens. Though I confess I was unusually tempted. Smythe was a beast to his wife."

"I always thought Diana deserved better."

It was Malcolm's turn to study Tommy. Diana Smythe, he suspected, harbored secrets. He profoundly hoped Tommy wasn't one of them.

"Speaking as an outside observer," Tommy said.

It sounded genuine. With Tommy, one could never tell. "I also had the sense Beverston never had much respect for his son."

"I'd say you're spot on there. Also that Beverston had about as much respect for him as John deserved."

"I hadn't thought—You must have known Smythe well."

"I've known him since we were in leading strings. In recent years, I've had as little to do with him as possible."

"Smythe said his father more or less saw him as cannon fodder. I imagine Beverston has rather more use for you."

"I like to flatter myself that he does. He gave that impression when he recruited me."

Malcolm studied his colleague—former colleague—again, trying to picture Tommy as a young man, throwing his lot in with the League. "And you thought—"

Tommy took a sip of brandy. "That the League had more to offer than the diplomatic corps. Or Carfax." Tommy regarded Malcolm for a moment. "We both went into diplomacy and intelligence for escape, Rannoch. But I was trying to escape boredom."

Past scenes shot through Malcolm's memory. Tommy dictating to him as they decoded an intercepted French dispatch. Hiding out together in the underbrush in the Spanish countryside, sniper fire on two sides. Copying out orders from Castlereagh in Vienna. "How long—"

"Stop looking at me like a snake, Rannoch. It's not as though I was trying to undermine us in the Peninsula. The League wanted Bonaparte defeated as much as Carfax and Wellington did. Unlike your wife." He studied Malcolm. "The conflict on your face is priceless. As it happens, I didn't know the truth about Suzanne—Mélanie—then. I didn't until quite recently. Though I may have learned it before you did."

Malcolm settled back in his chair and crossed his legs. "A number of people did. On the other hand, I know her in ways I don't believe anyone else does."

"Won't argue with you there, old boy." Tommy took another sip of brandy. "I always thought you were a bit mad to think you could make your marriage work. Agents really aren't suited for it. But you've managed better than I expected you would that day in Lisbon when you made her your wife. God, remember how stuffy the sitting room was? Having got this far, I can quite see how you'd have found a way past her betrayals. She's a woman worth hanging on to."

Malcolm fixed his gaze on Tommy's face. Belmont sounded uncharacteristically sincere.

Tommy gave a smile that looked faintly abashed. "I don't believe in love. But I can understand its allure. Even understand others wanting to continue as long as possible under the delusion that they've found it."

"Your romanticism knows no bounds, Belmont."

"I'll even go so far as to say your delusions may hold on longer than most. So, given all that, don't you want to bring Mélanie and your children back to Britain? For all Carfax accused you of not appreciating it, I think it means something to you. Rather more than it means to me, if it comes to that."

"If you know about Mélanie, you know perfectly well why we can't go back."

Tommy tilted his head to one side. "I'd have once sworn I'd never see you afraid of Carfax."

"I once didn't have a wife and children."

"All the more reason for you to want Carfax destroyed."

Malcolm locked his gaze on Tommy's the way he once would have on his opposing number at a diplomatic negotiation. "What are you offering, Tommy?"

"Help us bring Carfax down. We'll protect you from him. And with Carfax destroyed, you and Mélanie can live where you wish."

"Given the number of people who know about Mel, you can't imagine simply getting rid of Carfax would make us safe."

"It would certainly go a long way towards doing so. We have no wish to destroy either of you."

"You'd say that anyway. And even if it happens to be true, it's no guarantee of what may happen in the future."

"Fair enough. But Carfax is a clear threat now." Tommy watched Malcolm for a moment. "My God. After all he's done, you're still loyal to him."

"Don't be stupid, Belmont."

"I'm certainly capable of being stupid, but in this case I think I'm damnably acute. In all this time, you haven't moved against Carfax."

"I've been focused on protecting my family."

Tommy turned his glass in his hand. "He always complained your scruples got in the way. Whereas he knew perfectly well I didn't have any. But the funny thing is, you were always his favorite for all that."

"Carfax has known me since I was a boy, and he used that to play on my emotions when it suited him. That hardly made me a favorite."

"Oh, I don't deny he turned your childhood connection to his advantage, but it was more than that. I think a part of him admired you, while at the same time it drove him mad that he couldn't control you. I always used to think he wished you were his son instead of David."

"You have a keen understanding, Belmont, but now you really are being stupid. Carfax knows who his son is. He puts all too much pressure on David."

"And I'll even admit he cares about David. But I think Carfax would have liked a son with an affinity for the intelligence game. It must have cost him a lot to move against you."

"You know Carfax. He weighs the odds in every move he makes. And never looks back."

"Or doesn't admit he does." Tommy watched Malcolm a moment longer. "You were loyal to him."

"Too loyal for too long."

"My point exactly."

Malcolm leaned forwards, gripping the arms of his chair. "I'd like nothing better than to see Carfax removed from power. For reasons that are far more personal than I usually admit to, but also because he's a menace to Britain and the world. But not at the expense of empowering the Elsinore League."

"So sure you know them?"

"I know they're trying to kill my father."

He threw it out deliberately, to shock Tommy, and to see how much he knew. Tommy's eyes widened with surprise. But at the fact that Malcolm had spoken, not at what he'd said.

"It was hardly a great secret," Malcolm said. "And as I suspected, you already knew."

"But I hadn't expected to hear you claim him as a parent. Though given that he's living with you, I suppose I should have done. As I said, you're loyal to a fault."

"My relationship with O'Roarke goes beyond loyalty."

"He's a clever man. And a very dangerous one. Carfax and the League are both right there."

"Carfax and the League are both jumping at shadows when it comes to O'Roarke. Unless there's a great deal I don't know. Which, of course, is entirely possible."

"You don't sound very concerned."

"I'm not. I may be a fool, but I trust him."

Tommy shook his head. "You've always been a bit mad, Rannoch. All right. You view your wife's former spymaster and lover as your parent. What if I could offer to call off our efforts against him?"

"Why in God's name, would I believe that?"

"You don't believe in God any more than I do, Rannoch. But I could offer you guarantees."

"And what? If something happens to O'Roarke, I can revoke the treaty?"

"Surely you see the League would have reason to keep you happy so you'd assist them."

"And when they no longer needed our assistance? You put a knife in O'Roarke's ribs? Or mine? Or my wife's? How do I know all of this isn't just a ploy to get at O'Roarke?"

"You think he's more important than Carfax?"

"You tell me."

"Oh, no, Rannoch. You're not drawing me out that easily."

"So you know why they want him dead?"

"O'Roarke's been an enemy of the League for a long time."

"But they didn't start trying to have him killed until six months ago."

"That you know of."

"Of course, O'Roarke thinks it's more than half an excuse to reach out to Julien St. Juste."

"Who?"

"Spare me, Tommy. You're good at deception, but I can read you rather well."

"I was rather hoping he might turn out to be here."

"Why on earth would he be here?"

"Stranger things than that have happened."

Tommy had a point. Though not one Malcolm felt inclined to acknowledge. He bit back a bitter laugh at the thought of Julien St. Juste lurking about Dunmykel. Or simply sauntering in and asking to be shown to his room. "Who attacked you, Tommy?"

"I don't know."

"Is Carfax on to you?"

"Not that I know of. Are you planning to tell him?"

"I'd have to talk to him first."

"Stranger things than that have happened as well."

"You're safe under our roof, Tommy. After that, I make you no guarantees."

Tommy nodded. "It's more than I'd do for you."

"I'm not sure about that." Malcolm pushed himself to his feet. "You always had a certain loyalty. Though that was before I knew about your current employer."

"You don't have delusions you can hide in Italy forever, do you?"

"I expect I have a number of delusions, Tommy. But not about that."

"So you think you can take on the League and Carfax?"

"You always said I was a madman."

Tommy gave a soft laugh. "I always thought he knew just how brilliant you were and secretly regretted you weren't really his son."

"I told you, Tommy, whatever Carfax thinks of me, he never—"

"I'm not talking about Carfax." Tommy's eyes gleamed like agate in the candlelight. "I'm talking about Alistair Rannoch."

Chapter 11

"Good God." Mélanie looked up at her husband. "I don't know why I'm so surprised. It makes a certain sense. But I never thought—"

"Nor did I. I wouldn't have said I trusted Belmont, but I suppose in a way I did. At least to be more or less on the same side." Malcolm dug a hand through his hair. "You'd think I'd have learned not to talk about sides. And not that working for Carfax would put Tommy on the same side as us, in any case."

"You never worked for the League, though. There aren't the same reverberations."

Malcolm gave a short laugh. "Tommy accused me of still being loyal to Carfax. He's usually more acute in his perceptions."

"Tommy's annoying, but he's always been very acute." Mélanie studied her husband. The cool winter sunlight streaming through the leaded glass panes of their bedchamber window outlined the lean angles of his body but shadowed the sharp, Celtic bones of his face. "Darling. Carfax is still the man who befriended you growing up. Who gave you a purpose. There's no shame in not wanting him completely destroyed."

Malcolm twitched his shirt cuff straight, gaze on the linen. "Carfax gave me a purpose that went against everything I believed in. And the worst of it is, he didn't pull the wool over my eyes. In the end, I can't really blame anyone but myself. I know who he is and what he stands for. I'll say this for him, he never pretends to be other than he is. He's tried to destroy just about everyone I care about, but I don't want to see him in prison or executed as a traitor. If that's loyalty, then I'm guilty of still being loyal to him."

"No one should feel guilty for being loyal."

"That rather depends on what one's loyal to, as I think my father would say."

Mélanie regarded her husband steadily. "I think Raoul knows full well the damage that comes from going against personal loyalty."

"He knows one can't always be true to all one's loyalties. But mostly he's managed not to betray his ideals." Malcolm set his hands on her shoulders. "Part of me would like nothing better than to sit back and watch Carfax and the League destroy each other, but we can't afford to do that. Better tell the others."

"Obviously, this offer is even more absurd than Oliver's." Malcolm's gaze swept the company. Raoul, Laura, Cordy, Harry, Archie, Frances. "Though it might be a chance to learn more about the League."

"You've thought about pretending to make a deal with Belmont?" Harry asked.

"How could I not? But it would be a challenge to deceive Belmont."

"Since when have we not been up to a challenge? I'd like to think the two of us are a match for Tommy Belmont."

Laura cast a glance at Raoul. "You don't think—" Laura, usually so direct, didn't seem quite able to say it.

"That Belmont is here as an assassin?" Raoul reached for her hand and laced his fingers through her own. "He's a capable agent. But I think even he'd be slowed by his injuries."

"And we still don't know who inflicted those," Mélanie said.

"Could Carfax be on to him?" Cordelia asked.

"Possibly," Malcolm said. "Though one wouldn't think he'd have to wait until Tommy was this far away to strike."

"No, one wouldn't," Raoul said. "But if Carfax wasn't behind it, and we aren't, it leaves the interesting question of who else is a player in the game."

"Someone who didn't want Tommy to get here and approach us?" Mélanie asked. "Or who wanted to remove Tommy for other reasons?"

"Which could have to do with whatever else the League are plotting," Malcolm said.

"We don't know how long Belmont's been in the area," Harry said. "He could be the man who broke in and searched Lady Arabella's rooms."

"Quite." Malcolm met his friend's gaze. "Tommy's been to Dunmykel before. I just asked Gelly, and she remembers showing him the secret passage. I'd have said he'd cavil at shooting Mel, but now I'm not so sure."

"Whoever it was was firing a warning shot, not trying to shoot me," Mélanie pointed out.

"A warning shot dangerously close to you." Malcolm's fingers curled inwards. "Tommy could have been attacked because someone thought he found the papers. For that matter, he could really have found them. Or he could be back here to make another attempt to search. Though even Tommy will be hard pressed to do so for a bit."

"If you pretended to accept his offer and make a deal with the League, would you be able to learn more?" Cordelia asked. "And would it protect Raoul for a while?" She looked at Raoul. "Not that you aren't perfectly capable of protecting yourself."

"Spoken like a true diplomat, Cordelia," Raoul said. "But knowing the League, as Malcolm says, this could all be a ploy to get us off our guard."

A log fell from the grate, hissing against the fender. Malcolm moved to the fireplace. "All the more reason Grandfather and Talleyrand's plan won't work." He picked up the poker and pushed the log back into the fire. "Not that we could consider it in any case." The poker rattled as he returned it to the andirons. "Italy seems very appealing just now."

"On the other hand, this makes it harder to stay off the field," Raoul said. "Both Carfax and the League are going to seek us out wherever we go. The only solution is to fight back."

"Which we're trying to do," Mélanie said.

"This makes results more imperative." Archie was frowning into the fire.

Malcolm turned to look at his uncle-by-marriage. "It curtails what you can do with the League even more."

"I know." Archie looked at Frances.

"Don't tell me I have to immure myself in the Highlands until the babies are born," Frances said, with a horror that was only partly feigned. Her doctor son-in-law had detected a double heartbeat, but the knowledge that she was carrying twins was not enough to slow Frances down.

Archie gave a faint smile, though his gaze remained serious. "I'd hardly feel comfortable away from you at this of all times."

85

"So we both go back to London."

"Or we both stay here."

"Archie! We'd go mad."

"The League are afraid," Raoul said. "So is Carfax. Which puts us in a rather unique position."

"But doesn't make either any less dangerous," Malcolm said.

"Can Tommy tell them anything dangerous?" Cordelia asked.

"Anything he picks up here," Malcolm said, nudging a log with the toe of his boot. "Which, knowing Belmont, could be a lot, even wounded. And could be part of the League's strategy in sending him here in the first place."

"I don't suppose we could let him think we'd made an alliance with Oliver and Carfax, could we?" Cordelia asked.

"Not a bad idea," Raoul said. "If we could pull it off."

"I wonder—" Archie frowned.

"What?" Frances asked.

"Should we reconsider releasing a few names to Carfax? To keep the League on their toes. And throw Carfax off balance."

Malcolm nodded. "Loath as I am to have anything to do with Carfax, it's not a bad idea. And it might help draw Carfax out."

"So we're back to someone needing to meet with him," Harry said. "I may be the best choice."

Archie cast a sharp look at his nephew.

"I'm not important enough to be a target of the League," Harry said.

"Don't believe that for a minute, lad."

"And if it comes to it, Wellington still likes me," Harry said. "Besides, I haven't done anything that could be construed as treason. Which is more than could be said for most of the agents in this room."

"Point taken," Raoul murmured.

"Mind you, at this point I'd call being accused of treason a badge of honor," Harry added. "But my relatively blameless record is an advantage."

"So is mine," Cordelia said.

Harry drew a breath.

His wife turned to look at him. "Don't you dare suggest I stay behind."

"I wouldn't dream of it, sweetheart. But one of us should be in a position to get the girls back to Italy if it comes to it."

MIDWINTER INTRIGUE

"Damn you." Cordelia tucked her hand through her husband's arm. "I hate it when you're logical, darling."

Chapter 12

Harry glanced at the Yule log blazing in the old drawing room grate. "So it's settled. I'll leave for London after Boxing Day."

"You'll miss Hogmanay," Malcolm said.

"I'll have other chances for a Highland New Year."

Malcolm stared at the children playing in front of the hearth, their Christmas presents spilling off the hearth rug, on and about the sofa table and much of the drawing room carpet, and wondered when he'd have another chance for one himself. Hard, with everything that was going on, to remember to try to drink it in. Most of the family were here. His cousin Aline and her husband Geoffrey Blackwell and their daughter Claudia had arrived two days ago, in time for Christmas. Malcolm touched his friend's arm. "Thank you, Harry."

"It's all our fight," Harry said. "This is the obvious solution. But don't worry. I'll see you again soon, here or in Italy."

They moved to join the others by the fire. Cordelia smiled up at Harry over the back of the sofa where she sat. "Don't worry, I'm not going to argue more about staying. It doesn't mean I have to be happy about it. But I won't let it spoil Christmas."

Harry moved to stand behind the sofa, and lifted his wife's hand to his lips. "I'll be back before you know it."

Malcolm exchanged a smile with Mélanie, who was on the floor with Dorothée, dressing dolls, and then went over to Talleyrand, who was sitting in a wingback chair, observing the scene with a smile of unusual warmth.

"I'm glad you and Doro are here," Malcolm said, pulling a canvaswork chair up beside the prince.

"We're both enjoying it." Talleyrand's gaze softened still further as it went to his nephew's wife, her crimson velvet and black lace skirts spread on the floor about her and her dark ringlets spilling about her face.

"Doro's missed you both. I presume you won't let it get about if I confess I have as well."

"I wouldn't dream of betraying your secret," Malcolm said. He watched his wife for a moment. She had Berowne in her lap and was tying a bonnet on Jessica's new doll, her legs curled casually beneath the emerald green silk of her gown, one of the delicate shoulder straps slipping from her shoulder. Jessica observed with great concentration. Malcolm's gaze shifted to Raoul turning the pages of a book with Colin, Emily, and Livia grouped round him, then to Laura talking to Chloe over her new copy of *Pride and Prejudice,* Chloe's puppy curled up beside them. "You can't imagine how grateful I am for your offer. I know what you're risking, and it means the world to me. But you must understand why we can't accept it."

Talleyrand regarded him for a long moment with the shrewd gaze Malcolm remembered from childhood. "I understand why you *won't* accept it. The offer still stands. You need only send word from Italy or wherever you are. My ability to negotiate with Carfax and my willingness to do so won't change."

Malcolm touched the prince's hand where it lay on the carved arm of his chair. "Thank you, sir. Wherever we live, your friendship means a great deal."

The crowd moved and shifted. Archie came over to speak with Talleyrand. Malcolm moved back to the center of the room to hear Harry, now perched on the arm of the sofa beside Cordelia, saying, "While I'm gone, perhaps you can discover Arabella Rannoch's hiding place."

"I can't remember the last time I felt such a failure." Mélanie plucked a bit of fluff from a doll's cloak off the shimmering silk of her skirt.

"It's depressing." Frances twisted the sapphire bracelet Archie had given for Christmas round her wrist. "I used to be quite proud of my ability to read Arabella. Though looking back, there's certainly a great deal I missed."

"I can't believe we can't find it, if it's actually here in the house," Gisèle said from the floor, where she sat with Ian in her lap. "Andrew and I both grew up here, and we've been running the house for almost two years—"

Mélanie had gone still, her gaze on the flashing stones of Frances's bracelet. "What was it you were saying about Lady Arabella's jewelry, Andrew? That Gisèle and Lady Frances and Lady Marjorie have it? Gelly, is your mother's jewelry here? The pieces you have, at least?"

Gisèle met Mélanie's gaze. Without a word, she put Ian in Andrew's arms and ran from the room. She returned with her jewel box a few minutes later. "I know what you're thinking. But there's nothing large enough—"

"If there's one thing one learns as an agent, it's that looks can be deceiving." Mélanie lifted out a silver filigree locket set with pearls.

Malcolm stared at it, images of it round his mother's throat running through his memory. Could it be that simple? He moved to stand behind Mélanie, who was now sitting on the sofa, as she snapped the clasp open. His own face and those of his brother Edgar and Gisèle stared up at him. On the left, a miniature of him and Edgar, on the right one of Gisèle as a baby. Mélanie stared down at it for a moment, then ran her nail along the edge, snapped back the frame, and lifted out the picture of Malcolm and Edgar. A fragment of paper, tucked beneath, fell into her hand.

"Good God," Frances said. She, along with the others, had come to stand round the couch where Mélanie sat. "But where's the rest?"

Mélanie unfolded the paper to reveal an array of letters. Part of a code. The fragment of paper had obviously been cut from a larger sheet. When Mélanie took out the miniature of Gisèle, she revealed another fragment, though it didn't match with the first.

"May I?" Raoul reached over the sofa to pick up a necklace of pearls and amethysts from the jewel box. "I once saw Arabella use tweezers to put a stone back into a bracelet. If she was that good at replacing her jewels, it follows that she may have been equally good at removing them. If you'll permit me, Gisèle?"

Gisèle nodded. Raoul used a knife to pry out the largest amethyst. Another fragment of paper fell out into his hand.

Cordelia stared down at the sheet of paper Malcolm had set on the desk in the study, in the light of a lamp, for them all to see. His cousin Aline had spent most of the day decoding it, popping in occasionally to the Boxing Day celebrations with the tenants in the hall and drawing room to give an update or to say she was quite all right and it was much too interesting to ignore.

"Some of it's missing," Aline said now. "There must be more fragments hidden in jewels Mama or Aunt Marjorie have or that Mama gave to Judith or me. But I'm quite sure of what I have."

The wanderer securely bestowed. No further instructions necessary. Final payment may be left as promised—

She looked from Malcolm to Mélanie to Raoul to her mother. "Does it mean anything to you?"

"Not the words," Mélanie said. She was staring not at the decoded version, but at the pieced-together original that lay beside it. "But now that the letters are put together, I recognize the hand. It's Julien St. Juste's."

Frances stared from Mélanie to Raoul to Archie. "Why the devil would Arabella have been communicating with this Julien St. Juste two decades ago?"

"I don't know." Raoul's gaze was dark and even more hooded than usual. "And we don't know that they were in communication. Your story sounds more as if this is something Bella intercepted."

"Julien admitted to having had dealings with the League in the past," Mélanie said. "Lady Arabella could have intercepted something he sent them."

"Something that Carfax wants now." Malcolm put a hand on his wife's shoulder.

"Could he have learned about it from St. Juste?" Laura asked. "Perhaps it was part of the price for the papers St. Juste got back from him last June."

"Perhaps," Mélanie said. She was frowning down at the paper in a way that told Malcolm there was more she saw in it that she wasn't prepared to reveal yet.

"Harry," Frances said, "I'll give you a list of every piece of jewelry I received from my sister. You have my blessing to go into our London house and pull apart every piece. In fact, I shall be quite cross with you if you don't."

"I won't let you down, ma'am," Harry assured her.

They went back into the old drawing room where Andrew and Dorothée were keeping the children entertained. Mélanie dropped down on the hearth rug to play dolls, but Malcolm could see the concern lurking at the back of her eyes. Much later, when the children were in bed and they had retreated to their bedchamber with the core group of investigators—the two Davenport couples and Laura and Raoul—

Mélanie dropped down on the dressing table bench, arms folded across the claret velvet of her bodice.

"It's not entirely true that the words of the letter meant nothing to me," she said, accepting a glass of whisky from Malcolm. "Eight years ago, when Julien and I went into Switzerland with Hortense Bonaparte—" She took a sip of whisky, choosing her words carefully. All the others now knew that she and Julien St. Juste had helped Hortense Bonaparte conceal the birth of her illegitimate child, but Mélanie was still careful when speaking of it. "We stopped for dinner at an inn one night. Quite an adventure for Hortense to eat in the common room. Julien spotted someone watching us, and told Hortense and me to slip off to the stables. But on our way out of the inn, I rounded a corner and walked straight into a knife. Not my finest moment." Her fingers tightened on her arms. "They tied us up. But they didn't seem to know who Hortense was. They—there were three men—said we were the bait. What they wanted was Julien. Because he could take them to the Wanderer."

Malcolm drew a sharp breath. He glanced at Raoul, who had obviously heard the story before. His father's brows were drawn with concern.

"By the time Julien got there, I had my wrists free," Mélanie said. "Julien and I defeated the three men and got away with Hortense."

At another time, Malcolm would have given a great deal to learn how they had done so. But now he said, "And the Wanderer?"

"I asked Raoul later." Mélanie looked at her former spymaster. "You said you'd never heard of it."

"Which I hadn't," Raoul said. "Given the different masters St. Juste served, it could refer to anything. We don't even know if it's a person or a thing."

"Did you ask Julien St. Juste?" Cordelia asked.

"Yes." Mélanie took a drink of whisky and stared into her glass. "He said I was a thousand times better off not knowing.

Raoul touched his fingers to Laura's hair, spilling red gold on the white pillow, and slipped from their bed. Odd to feel such a bite of guilt, he thought, as he wrapped himself in his dressing gown. Guilt over acting in secrecy when that was how he'd lived his life for over thirty years. But in their nine months together, he and Laura had been amazingly open with each other. After all, they had begun their relationship knowing each other's deepest secrets. Or most of them.

He went down the passage and cast a quick glance about to make sure he was unobserved. Fortunately, though the footmen and grooms were still patrolling downstairs, after more than ten days without a further break-in, they weren't keeping as careful a watch upstairs. Raoul rapped at the door of Talleyrand's room. The prince opened the door promptly. He was in his dressing gown and nightcap, his wig on a stand on the dressing table, but his gaze said he'd been expecting Raoul's visit.

"Did you know?" Raoul asked, once the door was closed. He wasn't going to risk even that much until it was.

"That Arabella had papers concerning the Wanderer?" Talleyrand picked up a decanter from the escritoire and poured Raoul a glass of calvados. "No. I take it she never spoke of it with you?"

"I had no notion she even knew about the Wanderer." Raoul accepted the glass and took a drink. He needed it more than he cared to admit. "But what's more concerning at present is that apparently Carfax knows. And very likely the League as well."

"You think that's why they want St. Juste?" Talleyrand asked.

"It's occurred to me before. I hoped I was wrong. God help me, I hoped it was buried."

Talleyrand picked up his own half-full glass. "My dear O'Roarke, surely you realized long ago that nothing is ever really buried." He took a sip of calvados. For all the tranquility in his voice, his fingers were not quite steady. "I take it you haven't told your son? Or your daughter-in-law? Or your very charming mistress?"

"My God," Raoul said, "can you imagine I would?"

Talleyrand dropped into a chair by the fireplace and surveyed Raoul with a cool gaze. "The man you were the last time I saw you wouldn't have. But a number of things have clearly changed."

Raoul drew a breath, awareness of everything he'd gained in the past year and everything he risked sharp within him. "It's true I have few secrets from any of them these days. But some things are too dangerous to share."

Talleyrand's gaze drifted to the connecting door to Dorothée's room, then back to Raoul. "Which could prove complicated," he said. "Given that I don't think either of us is going to be able to stay out of this."

"No." Raoul tossed down the remainder of his calvados. His own words to Mélanie the night they'd arrived came back to him. *Good spies don't have ties.* "I don't imagine we will."

Mélanie closed the door of the night nursery. "I can't believe they're all finally asleep. Between Christmas, and Boxing Day, and their questions about the hidden message, I thought the chatter would never stop. Emily and Livia were pretending things were hidden in the paste necklaces we gave them."

Malcolm looked up from smoothing the covers over Jessica. She'd been sound asleep, draped over his shoulder, when he carried her upstairs an hour ago, before their conference about St. Juste. "She's managed not to roll over on the doll." The doll, which she'd named Rebecca, was tucked under the covers beside her.

"I told you, she's very careful for two." Mélanie came to stand beside him and slid her arms round him. "I don't know why, at this point, I'm surprised to find pieces of our worlds colliding. But I still can't quite believe your mother had a paper written by Julien."

Little more than a year ago, Malcolm had seen his mother as more of a tragic victim than a master player in the complex game they were all still caught up in. He had learned the truth about Arabella at the same time he learned the truth about Mélanie, and in some ways he was slower to adjust to it because Arabella wasn't here to face every day. He had no chance to talk to her and explore the reality of who she had been. He hesitated for a moment, because talking about Arabella still didn't come easily to him. Then he smoothed his wife's silky, dark hair back from her face. "I spent a decade trying to escape Arabella's memory. That was no answer. But I think I still have a tendency to view her as part of the past. When she's very much tangled up in our present."

"Whatever or whoever the Wanderer is, she was on to it." Mélanie's dark winged brows drew together. "And now both Carfax and the Elsinore League want it or him. Or her. Presumably to use against each other."

"And given Arabella's quest to expose the League, it seems most logical that hiding the Wanderer was an assignment Julien undertook for the Elsinore League that Carfax has got wind of. Though, considering he worked for both—and probably more for Carfax—it's possible it's the other way round. Either way, what's not at all clear is why Arabella hid the information away instead of using it."

"She obviously thought the papers vitally important and dangerous enough that she went to great lengths both to get them and to hide them. Either she was keeping them to use later, or—"

"Or she was protecting someone." Malcolm met his wife's gaze. "But clearly not Carfax or the League." He leaned forwards and brushed his lips across her temple. "I sometimes think I've learned more about my mother in the past year than in the two decades I lived with her. Yet, in many ways she seems more of a stranger than ever."

Malcolm pushed back the covers. New Year's Day. 1819. A new year, beginning with the same questions as the last. Harry should be in London soon, though it would be some time before they could expect any news. Folly to refine upon the frustrations of being out of the action. He could almost hear the sardonic comment Harry would make.

He shaved and dressed quickly. To his surprise, as he was putting on his coat, his wife sat up in bed, dark hair tumbling over her bare shoulders.

"You're up early," he said.

"Starting the new year off on a bright note. Don't place any reliance upon it lasting."

Malcolm grinned. "I should go down and see if Gelly and Andrew need help. I don't know how many callers we'll have today, or how early they'll arrive."

If they were in Edinburgh, midnight last night would have seen a parade of callers arriving to toast the New Year. In the country, with snow on the ground, they'd been limited to a handful from the nearest tenant farms, and Stephen Drummond and his family who had been the first over the threshold after midnight. But morning would probably bring more callers, and they were holding open house, much as they had on Boxing Day.

Mélanie petted Berowne, who had stretched and rolled over onto his back, and reached for her dressing gown. Jessica stirred in her cradle. "I should feed her," Mélanie said. "We'll be down soon."

Malcolm leaned down and kissed his wife. "Happy New Year, sweetheart."

Mélanie slid her fingers into his hair. "That's even better than our New Year's Eve kiss. Happy New Year, darling."

Malcolm went along the passage and down the stairs. Odd to be starting off the new year at Dunmykel. Odd, and for all the complications, surprisingly satisfying. Another memory to store up.

Voices carried up the stairwell. Too low to make out the words, but urgency underlay the tone. He quickened his pace and rounded the half-landing to see Andrew and Alec conferring near the front doors.

Both looked up at him. Andrew's face was pale, his gaze stricken. Malcolm bounded down the remainder of the stairs. "What is it? Is it Grandfather? Or Gelly?"

Andrew drew a breath, but he seemed beyond speech. It was Alec who answered, though his own face was drawn with concern. "The duke is well, sir. Mrs. Thirle left in a carriage early this morning. With Mr. Belmont."

Historical Notes

According to the historical record, Talleyrand and Dorothée did not visit Scotland in December 1818. Though if they had known the Rannochs, anything is possible...

Sneak Peek at THE DUKE'S GAMBIT

Out May, 2017

Chapter 1

Dunmykel, Scotland
1 January 1819

Malcolm Rannoch stared at the footman who had just told him his sister had left her home on a snowy New Year's Day with the agent of his enemies. "Mrs. Thirle got into a carriage with Mr. Belmont and drove off?"

"Yes, sir." Alec's gaze was wooden yet somehow at the same time sharp with sympathy.

"Did she say anything?" Gisèle's husband Andrew had been standing by in white-faced silence, but now his sharp voice cut the still air of the hall. "Give you a message?"

"No, sir." Alec hesitated. "They appeared to be in a hurry."

"Did she seem distressed?" Malcolm asked. "Were they—could Mr. Belmont have had a weapon pressed to her side?"

Alec hesitated again, shifting his weight from one foot to the other. "No, sir." Apology shone in his eyes and rang in his voice, as though he wished he could have claimed Gisèle was coerced. "They were conversing. They appeared to be in a hurry, but I saw Mrs. Thirle turn back to Mr. Belmont and—"

"What?" Andrew asked, voice taut with agony.

"She was laughing," Alec said, as though admitting to a glimpse of some terrible calamity. Which in a way he was.

"What's happened?" As if responding to a stage cue, Malcolm and Gisèle's aunt, Lady Frances Davenport, came down the stairs. She had Ian, Gisèle and Andrew's baby son, in her arms. Malcolm's wife Mélanie was just behind, holding their two-year-old daughter Jessica by the hand.

Andrew turned to the woman who had raised his wife. "Gelly's gone off in a carriage with Tommy Belmont."

In his thirty-one years, Malcolm had rarely seen his aunt's composure break to display shock or hurt. Now he saw both emotions flash across Frances's well-groomed features. "Did she—"

"She doesn't appear to have been coerced," Malcolm said.

On the step behind Lady Frances, Mélanie's gaze had also gone white. She picked up Jessica, as though to reassure herself, but her gaze went to Alec. "Did Majorie go with Mrs. Thirle?"

"No, ma'am," Alec said.

Marjorie was Gisèle's maid. Mélanie as usual was thinking clearly in a crisis. "Thank you, Alec," Malcolm said. "Perhaps you could ask Marjorie to join us in the library."

"Of course, sir. Right away."

Inside the library, Malcolm poured sherry, despite the early hour, and pressed it into everyone's hands. Andrew stared into his glass as though he wasn't sure what to do with it. Frances took a quick swallow, then pressed a kiss to Ian's forehead. "I take it she didn't leave any sort of note?"

Andrew shook his head. "Only last night we were talking about taking Ian sledding today. Either something changed very quickly or she's an actress on a level I never imagined—" He drew a sharp breath.

"It's possible," Mélanie said. "But Gisèle isn't a trained agent." Unlike Malcolm and Mélanie herself, and any number of their friends and family. Malcolm met his wife's gaze over their daughter's head. Jessica squirmed to be put down and walked over to investigate the chess set by the library windows.

"Andrew." Frances took another sip of sherry and fixed Gisèle's husband with a firm stare. "I'm sure I don't need to point out to you that Gisèle isn't her mother. Or her aunt."

Andrew gave a faint smile that didn't reach his eyes. "I'm sure Gisèle would quite like to be compared to you, ma'am. But she'd be the first to admit she's different."

"Well then." Lady Frances's tone was brisk. Perhaps a shade too brisk. "Having grown up with this family and been married into it for almost two years, I'd think you'd understand how often our behavior is inexplicable."

"And I'd be a fool to claim any insights?" Andrew said. "You make a good point, Lady Frances. But—"

Ian gave a squawk and kicked his legs against Frances's stomach.

"He's hungry." Andrew took his son from Frances's arms. As though in confirmation, Ian grabbed at the neck of Andrew's shirt.

MIDWINTER INTRIGUE

"I'll feed him." Mélanie held out her arms for the baby. "Jessica's old enough to share and I think I still have enough milk."

Andrew put Ian in her arms, as though the reminder that their son was still nursing made him realize just what Gisèle had walked away from. "I can't believe she—"

"We don't know what she's done." Frances put a hand on Andrew's arm. "Drink that sherry, you're going to need it."

Jessica looked up from the chess pieces as her mother took Ian, then went back to them without concern. Malcolm watched his wife settle Ian at her breast. Mélanie, one of the best agents he had ever met, who had spied on her own husband for years, had never spent the night away from either of their children. Which made Gisèle's actions even more inexplicable.

A rap sounded at the door and Marjorie slipped into the room. She was scarcely older than Gisèle. Her mother had been a housemaid at Dunmykel in Malcolm's childhood. Her red hair was pulled into a neat knot, but strands escaped about her face, as though she'd been tugging on them, and her nose was pink beneath her freckles as though she'd been crying. "I didn't know, Mr. Thirle. Mr. Rannoch. Mrs. Rannoch. Lady Frances." Her gaze darted round the company. "I swear it."

"No one's suggesting you did," Malcolm said. "Sit down, Marjorie. When did you realize Mrs. Thirle was gone?"

"This morning when I took in her tea." Marjorie moved to a chair and twisted her hands in her print skirt. "That is I saw she wasn't in her room. But I didn't think—"

"If she chose to get up early for some reason it wasn't your place to tell anyone," Malcolm said with a smile. "I quite understand."

Marjorie returned his smile, but her lips trembled "I never guessed—"

"Of course not," Mélanie said, rocking Ian in her arms. "Did she pack a bag?"

Marjorie gripped her hands together. "I didn't realize it at first. Not until after I learned she was gone. Then I looked and a small valise is gone with her nightdress and one gown and her dressing case. Nothing else."

Which made it less likely Tommy Belmont had pressed a pistol to Gisèle's side. Though it wasn't entirely beyond the realm of possibility for Tommy to have packed for her.

103

"I know you don't want to betray Mrs. Thirle's confidence," Mélanie said. "But had she seemed—distracted lately? Worried? Concerned?"

"No—that is—She'd had a lot to do with the holidays, of course. And with all the guests." Marjorie drew a breath as though realizing that referred to most of the people sitting before her. "She didn't say anything, but I think she'd been concerned about—"

"All the family issues," Malcolm said. Such as his grandfather's efforts to persuade him it was safe to come back to Britain despite the risks of Mélanie's past as a Bonapartist spy coming to light.

"Yes." Marjorie met his gaze directly. "But she was happy everyone was here. She was excited about Master Ian's first Christmas. When I helped her into her nightdress last night she told me Happy New Year. I can't imagine..."

Andrew, who had been staring at his hands, looked up as Marjorie's voice trailed off. "Did she ever say anything about Mr. Belmont?" He drew a rough breath. "I'm sorry, I know I'm the last person you must want to speak to about that. If it helps if I leave the room—"

"No." Marjorie shook her head. "I know Mrs. Thirle was worried about Mr. Belmont's wounds and relieved he was recovering, but I never heard her say anything to suggest she might—might leave with Mr. Belmont. She loves you very much, Mr. Thirle."

Andrew gave a twisted smile. "Thank you, Marjorie. I know how loyal you are to Mrs. Thirle."

Frances put a hand to her head, tucking a blonde curl firmly back into its pins. "There'll be callers arriving for New Year's Day in a few hours. And we have a house full of guests who will be down for breakfast soon. I'll try to put them off. If—"

She broke off as two of the guests filling the house stepped into the room. Raoul O'Roarke, who had once been Mélanie's spymaster and was also, Malcolm had learned a year ago, Malcolm's own biological father. And Cordelia Davenport, one of Malcolm and Mélanie's best friends, whose husband Harry was presently in London on a mission. Malcolm wasn't in the mood to waste time on explanations, but he welcomed both of their help, and their faces said they had already heard some of it.

"We asked Alec where Gelly was," Cordelia said, "and he said—"

"She left with Tommy Belmont," Andrew said. "We don't know why."

MIDWINTER INTRIGUE

"Good God." Cordelia glanced at Mélanie holding Ian. "Did she—"

They quickly brought Cordelia and Raoul up to date, Malcolm and Mélanie doing most of the talking. Malcolm saw the concern in Raoul's gaze though he said little. He knew more about secrets than any of them. He had also, like Frances, known Gisèle since she was a baby. And he knew about the Elsinore League, the shadowy organization Malcolm and Gisèle's mother had spent years trying to bring down, with Raoul's help, of which they had recently learned Tommy Belmont was a member.

Alec came back into the room. "Forgive me, sir. But the carriage has returned. Not with Mrs. Thirle," he added quickly, on a note of apology. "She and Mr. Belmont changed to a post chaise at the Griffin & Dragon in the village. They sent the carriage back. With a note for Mr. Thirle." He held a sealed paper out to Andrew.

Andrew was already on his feet. He took the paper at once, but stared at it for a long moment, as though breaking the seal could smash all his hopes to bits. Then he slit the seal with the opener Alec gave him, scanned the note quickly, and held it out to Malcolm without expression.

Andrew,

I'm quite safe, but there's something I have to take care of. I'll be back as soon as I can. Please don't come after me. Please, please do everything you can to keep Malcolm from coming after me. (I know that's almost impossible but try).

I'll write when I can.

Kiss Ian for me.

I love you.

Gelly

"It sounds like, Gelly," Malcolm said. "And it's her hand. It doesn't begin to explain." At a nod from Andrew, he handed it to Lady Frances.

"Why send a note now instead of leaving one when she left?" Cordelia asked.

"If she'd left a note, someone might have woken early and seen it," Malcolm said.

Alec gave a discreet cough. "According to the groom who returned the carriage, she left instructions to wait until the afternoon to return the carriage and deliver the note. But the staff at the Griffin & Dragon know her and decided not to wait."

"We should talk to the groom," Malcolm said.

Andrew nodded. "O'Roarke? Will you come with us? You're good at investigating things."

Raoul had been frowning at a glass-fronted bookcase as though it might hold answers, but he gave a crisp nod. "Certainly if you wish it."

Raoul hesitated a fraction of a second, as though searching for some way to give Andrew reassurance, then instead simply followed Andrew and Malcolm to the door. Malcolm understood.

Because given what they knew, there really wasn't any reassurance to give.

Lady Frances watched the men leave the room, an uncharacteristic line between her brows. In the cool January light, her rouge, usually expertly blended, stood out against her ashen skin. Mélanie had never seen her husband's aunt so shaken.

Frances cast a quick glance at Mélanie. "I'll talk to the others. You tend to Ian, my dear. Keep her company, Cordy."

She moved to the door, then turned back and touched her fingers to Jessica's hair. Jessica smiled up at her and went back to arranging the chess pieces. Frances's hand went to her own stomach for a moment. She was seven months pregnant with twins.

Mélanie swallowed, hard. When she woke this morning, before she learned of Gisèle's disappearance, she had already known they were confronting multiple crises, their friend Harry in London in search of information, their enemy Tommy Belmont seemingly recuperating upstairs from wounds from an unknown assailant, facing a return to exile themselves. But in the last two hours the world had shifted in ways she could still not yet fully comprehend.

"Look, Auntie Cordy," Jessica said. "The king and queen are getting married."

Cordelia dropped down beside Jessica for a few moments, her ruched cherry-striped skirts and lace-edged white petticoats billowing about her, then got to her feet and went to join Mélanie on the window seat. "Laura's with the other children," Cordy murmured to Mélanie. "She still doesn't know what's happened."

Laura Tarrington had been governess to the Rannoch children and now lived with them along with her own daughter. The children would be happy with her, though when they learned Gisèle was gone they were bound to have a flurry of questions Mélanie could not begin to think how to answer.

Cordelia looked at Ian. "I didn't want to say this in front of Andrew. But Gisèle left a baby. Who's still nursing. It can be a challenge even to leave a baby at home for an evening. One's body constantly reminds one of how long one's been gone even if one's head doesn't. She packed things to be gone over night at the least—"

"I know." Mélanie looked down at Ian, who had fallen asleep in her arms. "Some women fall into a depression when their babies are small. Usually earlier than this, but I've known women it's happened to months after the baby was born."

"But Gisèle wasn't depressed. We both saw her. Laughing on Christmas morning. Kissing Andrew at midnight only last night. I know she's Malcolm's sister, but I can't believe she's a good enough actress to have deceived us all about that."

"They're a talented family," Mélanie said, "but no, I wouldn't think so."

Cordelia regarded her for a moment. "What is it? Don't tell me you thought she was depressed."

Mélanie drew the folds of Ian's yellow blanket about him. "Not depressed. Preoccupied. Restless perhaps. When I first met Gisèle I don't think she saw herself as running an estate in the Highlands."

Cordelia laughed despite the situation. "When I was eighteen I didn't see myself married to a classical scholar and former spy and quite ready to turn my back on London society and live in exile."

"Cordy. You aren't—"

"Not yet, not precisely, but I wouldn't mind it in the least if we did. And I'm quite sure at eighteen you didn't envision yourself married to a British politician and living in Britain let alone going into exile in Italy with him. I doubt Laura saw herself as the mistress of a married revolutionary. I'm quite sure even a year ago Lady Frances didn't see herself married again and expecting twins. The point is life takes us unexpected places. Unexpected and often surprisingly happy places. I know it may sound odd coming from a woman who once ran off with another man, but I love my husband quite desperately enough to recognize the emotion in another woman."

Mélanie stroked Ian's hair. She saw Gisèle on her wedding day, "I do think she loves Andrew. But loving one's husband doesn't stop one from wanting other things in life. As I'm sure Mary Shelley would tell us."

Cordelia snorted. "Gisèle is much happier in her marriage than Mary Shelley."

"You've felt it, Cordy."

"Restlessness?" Cordelia wrinkled her nose. "I suppose so. Yes, all right, I have. Certainly when Harry and I were apart. Even now we're together. I love Harry. I never thought I'd love being a wife so much. I love being a mother. But it's not enough in and of itself."

"No. And nor is being a hostess or running a household. Even a household like Dunmykel."

"Yes, but I'd never leave Harry or my children—"

"Of course not. And we don't know that Gisèle intends to. At least not permanently."

Cordelia watched her for a moment. "You're very matter-of-fact about it."

Mélanie met her friend's gaze. "I'm not. I'm worried sick. But I'm trying damnably hard to think it through from Gisèle's perspective. Something has to account for what she did. And she doesn't appear to have been coerced."

Cordelia pleated a fold of her cherry-striped gown between her fingers. "They seemed so in love. Only a few days ago I was thinking—" She shook her head. "How fortunate Gisèle was to have found that sort of love the first time. Perhaps a part of me wanted to believe in the fairy tale."

"As I did. As I did with Bel and Oliver as well. But we of all people should know love is much more complicated than a fairy tale. "

Chapter 2

The groom who had brought the carriage and Gisèle's note back from the Griffin & Dragon was Rory Drummond, the younger brother of Malcolm and Andrew's childhood friend Stephen Drummond who had inherited the inn from his father a few years ago. The Drummond family had been at Dunmykel only last night, the first guests over the threshold at midnight.

"I'm sorry, Mr. Thirle, Mr. Rannoch," Rory said. Malcolm remembered Rory as a gangly teenager with spots. Now he was a young man past twenty, but his gaze was still bright and steady. "We weren't sure what to do."

"You couldn't have done otherwise," Andrew said. "Thank you for letting us know."

"Do you have any idea where they were bound?" Malcolm asked.

Rory shifted his weight from one foot to the other. They were in the slate-floored kitchen where Alec had brought Rory to have a cup of ale and warm up from the cold. "I confess I was concerned enough I was listening for clues. I heard Mr. Belmont say something about Glasgow. But I had the sense he meant me to hear it, if you take my meaning."

"Quite," Malcolm said. "Well done." Rory was an astute young man if he could outthink Tommy Belmont.

Rory's brows drew together. His blue eyes were dark with concern. "I wish—"

Malcolm touched his arm. "You've done well, Rory. Thank you."

He, Andrew, and Raoul left the kitchen but of one accord paused in the passage by the base of the service stairs.

"Where do you think they've gone?" Andrew asked.

"At a guess London," Malcolm said. "Though it's difficult to speculate without knowing *why* they've gone."

"We should look at Belmont's room," Raoul said. "Though I doubt he's left anything there."

The room in which Tommy Belmont had spent the past fortnight convalescing still smelled vaguely of Tommy's citrus shaving soap and the favorite brandy that he'd relied on to get past the pain of a serious chest wound. The blue-flowered coverlet was pulled neatly over the embroidered sheets. A dressing gown Malcolm had lent him hung from one of the oak bedposts. The dressing case Malcolm remembered standing on the chest of drawers was gone. Inspection of the wardrobe and chest of drawers also showed those bare. Malcolm and Raoul looked beneath things and tapped the paneling to be thorough, but Tommy was too seasoned an agent to have overlooked anything. Malcolm held the writing paper on the escritoire up to the light of the windows. "If he wrote anything, he managed not to leave an impression in the sheets below."

Raoul set down the poker after a fruitless examination of the ashes in the grate. "If he had, I'd think it was meant to mislead us."

"Quite," Malcolm said.

"You worked with Belmont in the Peninsula." Andrew was frowning at the leaded glass panes of the window. He'd only met Tommy Belmont once or twice before Tommy's recent unexpected arrival at Dunmykel.

"We were both attachés officially," Malcolm said. "And agents unofficially. At the Congress in Vienna as well."

"But now you've learned he's working for this Elsinore League you're all investigating." Andrew turned his gaze to Malcolm.

"Tommy admitted as much to me in this very room." Malcolm grimaced, wondering just what he had let into the house and all their lives when they gave shelter to Tommy. He had inherited Dunmykel with the death of his putative father the year before, but Andrew and Gisèle managed the estate and in many ways it was theirs. Malcolm had hoped it could be a haven for them away from the intrigues that engulfed the rest of the family.

"Do you think the League have something to do with why Gisèle left with Tommy?" Andrew asked.

"Did Gelly ever talk about them to you?" Malcolm kept his voice level, but he felt the tension that ran through Raoul. His mother had done her best to keep her children away from the League. Malcolm hadn't known of it himself until a year ago.

Andrew shook his head. "Only to say a few days ago that the more she learned about her mother, the more surprised she was."

"Do you think she could have been trying to discover more?" Raoul asked.

"I wouldn't have thought so." Andrew drew a breath. "Now I'm questioning everything I thought I knew about her."

For an instant, Malcolm was thrown back a year ago to the moment he'd discovered his own wife was a French agent who had married him to gather information. And that Raoul, who Malcolm had recently learned was his father, had been her spymaster and lover. He'd been sure he'd never trust anyone again.

"Gisèle has a good head on her shoulders," Raoul said. The faint roughness in his voice told Malcolm he was having some of the same memories. "And there's no reason to think Belmont intends harm to her."

"She always liked him," Andrew murmured.

"Andrew." Malcolm took a step towards his brother-in-law. "You read her note."

"She'd have written something like that no matter what," Andrew said. "I may not be a spy, but I can tell that much. She was doing her best to have us not follow them, though she probably knew there was little chance it would work." He met Malcolm's gaze. "I have to go to London. Or wherever else their trail takes me."

Malcolm, who had been determined from the moment three weeks ago when he stepped off the boat on the Dunmykel dock to get his family back to Italy as quickly as possible, inclined his head. "And I need to go with you."

"Damn it." Malcolm pushed the door to and took a turn about the bedchamber. "She wouldn't just disappear."

"Darling." Mélanie studied her husband's face, the tension in his jaw, in the set of his shoulders. They were alone in the room. Ian was asleep in the care of his nurse. Jessica was with Laura and Cordy and the other children while Cordy updated Laura on recent events.

"There has to be an explanation." Malcolm scowled at a Boucher oil of two young girls in a garden on the wall opposite. "She must have been coerced. If Carfax thought he could use her against us. Or the League—"

111

"Malcolm." Mélanie crossed to her husband's side and put her hands on his shoulders. "I'm as worried as you. But Tommy's with her." Whatever else one might say about Tommy Belmont, he could take care of himself and anyone with him.

"Precisely. So the League are probably behind it."

"That's one explanation."

"Mel, for God's sake—"

"It didn't sound as though she was coerced. And we have her note."

"Christ, Mel." Malcolm broke away from her hold. "You know as well as I do not to be taken in by appearances."

"Of course."

He stared at her. "But? What?"

"Only that we need to consider every possible explanation."

"I know. But she's my sister." He started pacing again. "You've only seen her a handful of times. I know her." He stopped short, staring at the Boucher oil again. "God, that's rich, I suppose, coming from the brother who abandoned her."

"Darling." Mélanie stepped up behind him and slid her arms round his back. "No one would say you abandoned her."

Malcolm gave a short laugh. "Gelly did. More than once. But I thought we'd mended matters."

"And you had. I saw you together. I saw her with Andrew and Ian. I'd have sworn she was happy."

Malcolm turned in her arms. His gaze darted across her face. "But?' His voice was gentler as he said it but inexorable.

Mélanie drew a breath. "I caught a restlessness sometimes. Nothing I could define. Nothing that made me think she intended anything. But in retrospect—"

"You're wondering if Gelly ran because you once thought about running?"

Mélanie held her husband's gaze with her own. "I never thought about leaving you, Malcolm."

"Never?"

"Only in the sense I knew I needed a plan if you ever learned the truth and tried to take the children away. But I know—"

"What?"

Mélanie drew a breath, seeing the flashes she'd sometimes caught in her young sister-in-law's gaze. Remembering moments from her own life as a London hostess. "What it's like to be happy in one's life and still be restless. To be happy but feel society's constraint."

A muscle tensed beside his jaw, but he merely gave a crisp nod. "Darling, I'm not—"

"I know. You'd never run out on your responsibilities. I suppose one could argue Gelly's a bit less responsible than you. At least she was. She was still throwing tantrums when you were an agent stealing papers from the ministry of police. I'd have said she changed. It could be argued that I wanted her to have changed. That I wasn't the best judge." He scraped a hand over his hair. "But Tommy was wounded and here on Elsinore League business. Even granted he wouldn't cavil at much, it's hard to see him as bent on seduction."

"No," Mélanie agreed. "Unless it was part of his mission."

"To use Gelly against us?" Malcolm drew a hard breath. "That I confess has the ring of the League. And Tommy. But how—"

"They might want to get you to London."

"And I'm playing right into their hands? But I don't see how I can do otherwise but follow her." Malcolm's gray gaze settled on her own, at once determined and tender. "I need to leave for London with Andrew at once."

Mélanie nodded.

Malcolm stared at her. Usually any suggestion that he take action without her met with quick resistance.

"Andrew will need your help and support. I don't want to leave the children, and you'll travel more quickly without us." Mélanie put her hands on her husband's chest. "Besides, you're in relatively little danger in London. I'm the problematic one."

His brows drew together. "If you get the least hint you're unsafe here—"

"I can pack up the children and go back to Italy. Don't worry, darling. I don't like to run, but I've never been afraid to when the situation calls for it."

"Ha."

"Seriously, darling. I may be reckless, but I've never been foolhardy. I wouldn't have survived in the game this long if I was. I'll pack a valise for you. If you need more you can get it from Berkeley Square. Valentin will be there. Assuming the trail takes you to London."

Malcolm nodded. "We're taking Andrew's curricle, it will be faster. We'll change horses at the first posting house and send his team back." He put his hands over her own and gathered them into a hard clasp. "This is serious. I know we've said that before. But this may be the most serious foe we've ever faced."

"We're equal to it."

Chapter 3

The room known as the old drawing room was unexpectedly quiet after the chaos in the house that morning. Most of the guests had retreated to their rooms. Cordelia had gathered the children in the library for charades. Laura Tarrington found herself alone with her lover for the first time since the news of Gisèle's disappearance. She walked up beside Raoul and slid her hand into his own. They had been lovers for almost a year and she was five months gone with their child, but long before that Malcolm and Gisèle's mother Arabella had been his lover for twenty years. "I know you must be desperate to be doing something."

He had been frowning at the mullioned panes of the window, but he turned his head and gave her a faint smile. "I'd only complicate things if I went to London with Malcolm and Andrew. I'm not sure what they're facing, but they're likely to need to move in London society." His gaze went back to the window. His brows were drawn, his mouth set, his gray eyes haunted in a way they only got in unguarded moments. "I keep seeing Gisèle toddling across the lawn holding Malcolm's hand. Or at seven with a grubby face and one of Arabella's coronets on her head. I always thought Arabella must have been a bit like that as a girl. Before her life got unbearably complicated."

"I hadn't thought somehow—that you'd have watched her grow up."

"Not as much as Malcolm, but I saw a fair amount of her. I remember carrying her about on my shoulders the way I do with Emily and Jessica now."

"Darling." Laura turned to face him and tilted her head back to look up at him. "Do you know who Gisèle's father is?"

"No," he said, without hesitation. "Only that it wasn't Alistair."

Laura drew a breath. But some things she'd once have shied away from she could now say. "It couldn't—"

Raoul looked down at her with that reserved tenderness she'd come to know so well. "I've always been fond of Gisèle, but if she were my daughter don't you think she'd mean to me what Malcolm does?"

"Of course. I just—"

"Wondered if I wasn't sure? It's true there's a great deal I don't know where Arabella's concerned, but we weren't lovers from before my marriage in '95 until after the Uprising in '98, well after Gisèle was born. There's no way I could be her father. Arabella could be frank about her love affairs—sometimes franker than I'd have wished—but she said nothing about her pregnancy save that it was unexpected."

"Do you think—could that have something to do with why Gisèle left? Searching for her father? Or because she learned who he was? We now know Tommy Belmont was working for the Elsinore League—"

"And Gisèle's father might have been a member? It's possible. Arabella did employ seduction in her attempts at gathering information."

As Mélanie had done. As Raoul had himself, Laura knew.

Raoul glanced at the Broadwood grand pianoforte. It had been Arabella's instrument, and this room, less formal than many of the rooms at Dunmykel, was one of her favorites, according to what Laura had heard from the family. "Bella was secretive over Gisèle's parentage. Unusually so."

"Especially with you."

His mouth lifted in a faint smile. "She didn't tell me everything. Far from it."

Laura put her hands on his chest. "Does Frances know who Gisèle's father is?"

"I don't know. I've never asked her. Though I think perhaps I have to now." He was silent for a moment. "Gisèle has a quick temper. She was always more mercurial than the boys. I know Frances worried about her growing up, but I never saw any sign that she'd inherited Arabella's illness."

"Even if she had, it wouldn't make her suddenly run off and leave her family."

"No," he said. "But something did."

MIDWINTER INTRIGUE

Raoul rapped at Frances's door and at her subdued summons stepped into the room to find her sitting on her dressing table bench, staring at a silver-framed miniature as though pleading for answers. Raoul had known Fanny since she was fourteen and he'd never seen such a lost look on her face.

She looked up and met his gaze. "Only last night she was talking to me about the babies and how wonderful it would be that they could play with Ian. I should have seen—"

"None of us saw," Raoul said, leaning against the door panels.

"But I'm—"

"Her mother to all intents and purposes. And she couldn't have a better one."

Frances shook her head. "Don't talk reassuring twaddle, my dear. We've known each other far too long."

"It's the truth. I don't think anyone else could have raised Gisèle as you did after Arabella died."

Fanny gave a bleak smile. "I love her as much as my other children. I may worry about her more. Difficult not to when Arabella—"

She broke off, but there was really no need to put it into words. They were both all too familiar with Arabella's brilliant intensity and bouts of depression. "Gisèle could be moody," Raoul said. "But I never saw any sign that she suffered from Arabella's affliction."

"No," Frances said, "nor did I. I tried hard not to drive her mad watching for signs of it." She looked down at the miniature again. "The past two years I worried less about her than I have since Arabella died." She shook her head. "Malcolm twitted me on it once, being happy when they all got married and had babies. And God knows I don't think that's the only path to happiness. Even now I've risked it again myself." She spread her fingers over her rounded stomach. "But it is one sort of happiness. And I thought Gisèle was genuinely happy with Andrew."

"I think she was." Raoul pushed away from the door and dropped down on the carpet in front of Frances. "Fanny, did Bella ever tell you who Gisèle's father was?"

Frances's eyes widened. "You've never asked before."

"No," he said, his gaze steady on her own. "I didn't think it was any of my business. But now—"

"You think that's why Gisèle ran off? Because she's trying to learn who her father is?"

"It's one possibility. Something made her run. With Belmont. I know Andrew's fears, but I doubt she's fallen in love with Tommy

117

Belmont. She could think Belmont can make it easier for Malcolm and Mélanie to return to Britain, but she's sensible enough I think she'd be likely to confide in Malcolm if that was the case. But if she thought he might know who her father was—"

"You're suggesting her father might be an Elsinore League member?"

"Do you think he might be?"

Frances's fingers tightened on the silver filigree frame of the miniature. Raoul could see the image now, Gisèle at about sixteen, her mother's sharp cheekbones just starting to emerge from round-faced girlhood, her eyes Arabella's brilliant blue, her honey-blonde curls a darker version of her mother's. Whoever her father was, the resemblance wasn't obvious.

"She never told me," Frances said. "Bella never told me who Gisèle's father was. Mind you, I didn't tell her who the fathers of all my children were. At least I don't think I did." Frances's penciled brows drew together. Of her five children, only the eldest had been fathered by her late husband. "But I confess I was curious. After all she told me right away with Malcolm, even though I was not yet fifteen, and she was very direct about Edgar being Alistair's. I'm a firm believer in everyone's right to secrets, but one night after we'd come home from the theatre and were drinking whisky together, I asked her straight out about Gisèle's father. Bella went still in that way she would sometimes. Then she laughed, almost as though she was laughing at herself, and said it was much better for me not to know." Frances linked her hands together over the curve of her stomach. "Of course at the time I didn't know about the Elsinore League. I didn't know a lot when it came to Arabella."

"Nor did I if it comes to that." Raoul sat back on his heels. "Did Gelly ever ask you?"

"Once when she was about fifteen. I told her honestly that I didn't know. She just nodded and said she supposed it didn't much matter. But there was a look in her eyes—" Frances shook her head.

Raoul laid his hand over Frances's own. "Did Alistair ever ask you?"

Frances went still. Arabella and Alistair Rannoch had been estranged for most of their married life, but Alistair had been Frances's lover for two decades. "Alistair rarely talked to me about Arabella. He had that much delicacy. But he did ask me once, when Bella was pregnant with Gisèle, in the most detached sort of voice, if I had any idea who the father might be. And of course I told him no. And that if he really wanted to know he should ask Bella."

Despite everything Raoul found himself giving a wry smile. "And?"

"He said he didn't suppose it much mattered. Much as Gisèle later would. But I'm not sure either of them meant what they said. If—"

She broke off, as the door opened to admit her husband, Archibald Davenport. Archie hesitated on the threshold. "Sorry, I can—"

"Nonsense." Frances pushed herself to her feet and went to take her husband's hand. "I won't go so far as to say we none of us have secrets from each other, because at our age, with our lives, we know that's not true, but in this we're all united."

Archie lifted his wife's hand to his lips. "You've both known Gisèle far longer than I have."

Raoul pushed himself to his feet. Fanny and Archie were two of his closest friends, and he was a man with few he'd call friends. "Did Arabella ever say anything to you about Gisèle's father?"

Archie raised his brows. "Surely if she didn't say anything to either of you—"

"Bella and I were franker with each other than many lovers, but still not entirely frank. And she was keeping the Elsinore League from Fanny."

Archie's brows drew together. "You think Gisèle's father may be a member of the League?"

"It's one possible explanation for why she's run off with Belmont."

Archie's frown deepened. He'd been a League member himself for years, but early on he'd grown concerned by their ambitions and had begun passing information to Arabella and to Raoul and then had moved on to passing information to Raoul about Ireland and France. "It's no secret to either of you that her investigation into the League sometimes took on intimate aspects. But she said nothing to me. And I can't remember anything from round the time Gisèle would have been conceived that would suggest who her father might be."

"Archie," Frances said. "This changes things."

Archie looked down into his wife's eyes. "You want to go back to London."

"I have to. It's all very well to worry about safety, but—"

"Of course." He pressed a kiss to her forehead. "We won't travel with Malcolm and Andrew and slow them down, but we can leave ourselves tomorrow."

Frances tilted her head back to look up at her husband. "Thank you."

"My darling, I could hardly do otherwise."

Malcolm found his father back in Tommy's room, tapping the paneling round the fireplace where they had already searched. Raoul turned to him with an abashed smile. "Trying to make one more search for clues."

"As I suspected you would be." Malcolm pushed the door to. "Andrew and I are leaving within the hour. For London or wherever their trail takes us."

Raoul nodded. "I assumed you would be as soon as we heard Gisèle was missing."

Malcolm scanned his father's face in the cool light from the window. Raoul wasn't one to stay out of things, any more than Mel was.

Raoul gave a faint smile. "Of course I want to go with you. I want to do anything I can to help. But I'd only create complications."

"Mel's agreed to stay. Which surprised me even more." Malcolm drew a rough breath. He knew what he had to do. And doing it was one of the hardest things he'd ever done. "I have no idea how long I'll be gone. And I'm leaving nearly everyone I love under this roof."

"It's far from ideal." Raoul spoke in the crisp tones of a commander acknowledging a risky battle plan. "But Mélanie should be safe here, especially while the winter weather holds. And if necessary we can be on our way to Italy quickly."

"I know you must need to get back to Spain." Malcolm recalled the taut urgency of his father's letters from Spain, where rebellion against the Bourbon monarchy was brewing and Raoul was in the process of setting up a network.

"My dear Malcolm. Mélanie and Laura are perfectly capable of getting the children to Italy on their own, as both would be the first to tell you, but you can't imagine I'd leave before this is resolved."

"You're running a network."

"I've made arrangements."

Malcolm met his father's gaze for a long moment. "Thank you."

MIDWINTER INTRIGUE

Raoul nodded, face contained. As often, much between them remained unspoken.

"Malcolm." Raoul hesitated, fingers taut on the mantel. "I can't claim to know Gisèle as you do. But I saw a fair amount of her growing up. It strikes me that one reason for her seemingly inexplicable departure might be that she thinks Belmont can help her find her father."

Malcolm's gaze locked on his father's. The thought had been there at the back of his mind, to the extent he'd had time to analyze at all, ever since he heard of Gisèle's departure. "I've thought of it," he said. "Especially since in Italy she realized I'd finally learned conclusively who my father is. That might have made her more curious to find her own."

"It's not me," Raoul said. "There's no way it could be."

"I didn't think it was," Malcolm said. "That is, I know you and Arabella were apart during your marriage to Margaret, and—" *Presumptuous to say, I know you're fond of Gisèle but it's not like what's between us.*

Acknowledgment flickered through Raoul's gaze. "Arabella also never gave me any indication of Gisèle's father's identity. I just asked Fanny and apparently the one time she asked, Bella told her she was much better off not knowing."

"You think it's someone in the Elsinore League?" Malcolm asked.

"I think it's a possibility. More to the point, Gisèle might think it's a possibility. And that Belmont could help her."

"And Tommy could be playing upon that because he and the League have other reasons for wanting Gisèle."

Raoul's mouth tightened. "It's possible. It's all still only a theory."

Malcolm looked into the gray eyes he now knew were the twin of his own. "I never thought I'd have to ask you this. But I'm going to need a list of Arabella's lovers who were members of the Elsinore League."

Raoul reached inside his coat and drew out a folded sheet of paper. "The names of all those I know of, and what I know about dates. There could well be others I don't know about."

"Thank you." Malcolm had never been so grateful for Raoul's matter-of-factness, and for the fact that he'd written the list down instead of Malcolm having to question him.

121

Raoul gave a crisp nod. "The dates aren't right for any of them to be Gisèsle's father. But Arabella could have been involved with one before I realized or resumed the affair later."

Malcolm tucked the list into his own coat. "The papers we found that Arabella had hidden in her jewels mentioning the Wanderer. Gisèle would have been a baby when Arabella hid them. Could they have anything to do with her father?"

Raoul's brows drew together. "The timing's right, but it's difficult to see how. Bella seems to have intercepted the papers. Likely from the League though we can't be sure. Whoever or whatever the Wanderer is, it's unlikely it has to do with Gisèle's parentage."

"No, but the man she took the papers from could be Gelly's father."

Raoul's eyes narrowed as though he was sifting through the facts. "She took the papers from her lover, then climbed out the window and back in through Fanny's room so it would seem like she came from outside? It's possible. In fact it sounds damnably like Bella."

"It's still only a theory, as you say." Something to ponder on sleepless nights in inns as he and Andrew tracked Gisèle and Tommy Belmont. Malcolm moved to the door, but turned back, his hand on the door knob. "Father? I couldn't leave as easily if you weren't here."

Raoul went still. Only then did Malcolm fully realize what he'd said. He gave a faint smile. "I've never said it, have I? I've thought of you that way for some time. But it's what I called Alistair. So I didn't—But damn it, I'm not going to let Alistair own a word you're much more entitled to."

"My dear Malcolm, that means—a great deal." Raoul drew a breath like that of a man stepping onto uncharted ground. "Now find your sister and try not to worry about the rest of us."

Chapter 4

Mélanie carried the valise she'd packed for Malcolm downstairs. She found Andrew in the study writing with a quick hand. "Malcolm's gone up to speak to the duke," he said. "I'm just writing out instructions for Tim." Tim Gordon was Andrew's assistant in running the estate. "He's been in charge before when Gelly and I've been in London." Andrew set down the pen. "You saw a fair amount when you and Malcolm visited in the past couple of years. Obviously you can speak for Malcolm in his absence."

"I'll do my best," she said. Running a large estate was far outside her field of expertise. On the other hand, when she married Malcolm she hadn't known anything about managing a large household or being a diplomatic and political hostess, and she'd become quite adept at both.

Andrew nodded and sealed his letter for Tim. Mélanie set down the valise and moved to a shield-back chair beside the desk. Andrew's drawn face and the set of his shoulders betrayed the appalling strain he was under. But her investigator's instincts had been racing ahead from the moment they learned Gisèle was missing. This was her last chance to put those to use. And to ask questions Malcolm might not be prepared to ask.

"Andrew—" Mélanie hesitated.

Andrew set down the Dunmykel seal and studied her, his face gray in the morning light. "You're wondering if I'm not telling you something."

"Of course not. I know how you feel about Gisèle. It's plain you're desperate to find her."

"But you're wondering if I knew she was unhappy. If I have some reason to suspect she might have run off."

The torment of doubt in one's spouse. For all they had battled through to, neither she nor Malcolm was a stranger to it. "I saw you and Gelly together. Unless I've completely lost my ability to read people, you love her and she loves you." She could see them on their wedding day, Andrew at the altar, dumbstruck with wonder, Gisèle on Malcolm's arm, radiant with joy. "I also know love is a complicated thing. So is marriage."

Andrew glanced through the mullioned panes of the windows at a snow-flecked line of birch trees. "I still remember the moment I looked at her and realized she wasn't my friend's little sister anymore. That first evening I kissed her. She was wearing a white wool cloak and snowflakes dusted her hair." He drew a harsh breath. "I'm thirteen years older. I should have known."

"Not to let yourself fall in love?"

"It was too late for that. On my side at least. But I took shocking advantage of her. She'd scarcely had a season. Scarcely had a chance to explore her options."

"As I heard it, you insisted Gisèle go back to London and go about in society for months before you'd let her commit to anything. Gelly claimed you were so scrupulously honorable it drove her mad, but at the same time that she loved you for it."

Andrew gave a twisted smile. "None of which changes the fact that in the end I gave way to impulse and let her tie herself to me when she'd seen little of the world and was far too young to be sure of what she wanted."

"I imagine Gisèle would say growing up in this family she'd seen a great deal of the world. And as I recall she was quite sure she wanted you."

"At the time." Andrew glanced out the window again, the look in his blue eyes both sweet and wistful. "And after. But it's damnably hard at eighteen to know what one wants for the rest of one's life."

"I was nineteen when I married Malcolm."

Andrew met her gaze across the oak and leather and chased silver of the desktop. He knew something of her past now, but not the full story. At least, she and Malcolm were convincing themselves he and Gisèle hadn't worked it all out. "You'd been through more than Gelly had," he said.

Mélanie studied him. "I think perhaps you're having one of Malcolm's over-protective moments. Perhaps having known Gisèle since she was a child you find it hard to believe she's grown up."

Andrew gave a bleak smile that nevertheless told of past joys. "Believe me, I'm very aware she's grown up."

MIDWINTER INTRIGUE

"In some ways. But perhaps in others you aren't giving her enough credit. *You* haven't changed since you married. Why should she?"

"I was older. I'd seen more of the world. And I suppose—" He returned the cap to the sealing wax with unwonted care. "A part of me could never quite believe she loved me."

"I know something about that."

Andrew's gaze shot to her face. "For God's sake, Mélanie. It's plain Malcolm adores you."

"Malcolm's not the type to adore. I do think he loves me. But that doesn't stop the thoughts about 'what if he sees the real me?'"

"My dear girl." For all his own crisis, Andrew's face was warm with concern. "You have nothing to worry about."

"Relationships can be so precariously balanced. For a long time I don't think I gave Malcolm enough credit. Perhaps that's what you're doing with Gisèle."

He watched her for a moment. "You're kind, Mélanie. And remarkably reassuring. But I know what you've been thinking. You can't help but wonder. Malcolm doesn't like to think it about Gelly. I don't think Lady Frances and O'Roarke do either. But you saw the possibilities at once."

"Seeing the possibilities doesn't mean I believe them."

"But you don't think we should ignore them."

"I think we need more information. But whatever Gisèle's done, I'll never believe she doesn't love you."

"And yet I think you're well aware of just how complex love can be."

"And what it can endure."

Andrew drew a hard breath. "Surely there are things you want to ask me. Things Malcolm wouldn't ask."

Mélanie swallowed. But she had wanted to seize her chance. This was it. "Did you have any reason to think Gisèle was unhappy?"

"Unhappy? No. If I'd thought that I'd have—" He shook his head. "I'm not sure what. Tried to fix it somehow. Asked her. But she's seemed—" He drew a breath as though fumbling for words the way he might hunt for a lost toy under the sofa. "Preoccupied. I'd catch her in unexpected moments, staring off into space. And then she'd turn to me with a bright smile as though she hadn't a care in the world."

Mélanie knew that look all too well. It was one she gave Malcolm loweringly often.

125

Andrew returned the pen he'd been using to its silver holder. "I thought she might be worrying about Malcolm and you. And not want to talk about it because perhaps Malcolm had confided in her but not in me. Which I'd understand. But it went on after you came here. And she seemed—restless somehow." He looked up quickly and met Mélanie's gaze before she could armor herself. "You saw it too."

"Perhaps. It could mean a lot of things. I'm restless at times myself."

Andrew aligned a stack of writing paper on the ink blotter. "Gelly loves Dunmykel, but I don't know that she'd ever have chosen life here on her own. It's yet another reason I worried about her marrying me too young. She grew up in London, in Lady Frances's household. She could have reigned over society like her aunt. Like her mother."

"Gisèle isn't Frances or Arabella. In any way."

Andrew settled a bronze paperweight on the writing paper. "She told me once Dunmykel was a haven. The place she'd been happiest as a small child and was happiest now. But I'm not sure a haven is a place one wants to stay forever, all the time. Not if one has Gelly's appetite for life."

The villa shot into Mélanie's memory. White walls. Tile floors. Flowers spilling over the balustrade. A sense of being cut off from the world that was at once soothing and terrifying. "Wanting more from life doesn't mean wanting life away from you."

Andrew drew a breath. When he spoke, she had the sense he was at last voicing a fear he'd been terrified to utter. "Gelly always liked Belmont."

Innocuous words. Which turned a phantom hanging in the air into a tangible reality, hovering before them. "With this family," Mélanie said, "the obvious explanation very often isn't the correct one."

"Very often," Andrew agreed. "But not always."

Malcolm found his grandfather, the Duke of Strathdon, in the sitting room of the suite the duke occupied on his visits to Dunmykel, pacing the floor. In his one-and-thirty years, Malcolm could not recall a time he had seen his grandfather pace.

"Wanted to stay downstairs," the duke said, turning to the door as Malcolm came into the room. "Had some illusion that I could be doing more at the heart of the house. But thought it would be easier for us to talk here."

"Thinking like an agent, sir." Malcolm advanced into the room. "My compliments."

Strathdon waved a hand, brows drawn together. "You think they've gone to London?"

"That's my best guess from the way they tried to obscure their trail. I could well be wrong. But I think I'll be able to read clues along the way. Tommy's good at covering his tracks, but I'm more than passably good at uncovering them."

Strathdon gave a crisp nod. "Why the devil—"

"I don't know, sir." Malcolm clasped his hands behind his back. His fingers were taut with strain. "At a guess I'd say she thinks she can do something to help Mélanie and me return to Britain."

Strathdon's frown deepened. "She didn't know my plan. Not the whole of it. I wanted to keep her out of it."

"So did I. But that may only have piqued her interest." In fact, three weeks ago, on the night of Jessica's birthday, Gelly had expressed her frustration to Malcolm at all the family secrets she didn't know. A conversation which in retrospect haunted him. "It's folly to blame yourself, sir," Malcolm said. "More information may have made her more inclined to involve herself." He hesitated a moment, but his recent exchange with Raoul echoed in his head. "O'Roarke and Aunt Frances also think it's possible Gelly's searching for information about her father."

Strathdon went still.

"You knew Alistair wasn't her father," Malcolm said. It wasn't quite a question.

"Credit me with a bit of sense, lad. By the time Gisèle was conceived I'd have been shocked if Arabella and Alistair got within ten feet of each other, let alone close enough to make a child."

"But you don't—"

"Good God, Malcolm. You can't imagine Arabella would have confided such a thing to me. Or that I'd have asked."

"That doesn't mean you didn't have suspicions. You did about my father."

Strathdon met Malcolm's gaze, his own blue eyes more open than usual. "True enough. But what was between your mother and O'Roarke was fairly obvious." He hesitated, glanced at the fire in the grate for a moment, coughed, looked back at Malcolm. "I don't think—"

"O'Roarke and Mama were apart when Gelly was conceived. He doesn't know who Gelly's father is. Nor does Aunt Frances. She says Mama told her not to ask."

Strathdon's gaze clouded, genuine concern overlaying the awkwardness of the subject. "You know I always let my daughters go their own way, for better or worse. One can argue I should have paid more attention—"

"Arabella was very good at keeping secrets however hard you'd have tried. This may have nothing to do with why Gelly's disappeared." Malcolm hesitated, then touched his fingers to his grandfather's arm. "I know how difficult it can be to wait, but I beg you, try not to worry too much, Grandfather."

"Don't waste your energies on me, Malcolm," Strathdon said, in more of his usual tones. "I may have pretended to ill health to get you back from Italy, but I am perfectly fit and hardly likely to be overset by worry. However serious the situation. I may not be an agent, but life in this family has taught me to expect the unusual."

"That I know full well, sir." Malcolm held his grandfather's gaze. "Mélanie, O'Roarke, and Laura may have to take the children back to Italy before I return. Should they think it necessary to do so, I pray you do everything you can to assist them."

"My dear boy, we may disagree on the possibility of your returning to Britain, but I would hardly attempt to stop your wife or your father or the charming Lady Tarrington from doing what they thought they must. Not that I have any illusions I could do so if I tried."

"No. Though I wouldn't care to put it to the test."

Strathdon's gaze flickered over Malcolm's face. "You'll be safe in London?"

"You were convinced enough I should be able to go back there."

"Talleyrand hasn't tried to bargain with Carfax yet."

"There's no evidence Mel's past is generally known. Even if it were, it doesn't implicate me unless they think I was working with her. And even in the worst case, it wouldn't be the first time I've got out of enemy territory."

The duke continued to frown. Malcolm touched his arm again. "Don't look so grave, sir. You've got your wish. I'll be on British soil a bit longer." He hesitated a moment after he said it, aware of the sudden rigidity of his fingers on the dark blue cassimere of his grandfather's coat sleeve.

MIDWINTER INTRIGUE

Strathdon's brows snapped together in a very different way from his frown of concern a moment before. "You think Gisèle and I orchestrated this to get you and Mélanie to stay in Britain?"

"The thought could not but at least occur to me, sir."

"By God." Strathdon ran a hand over his smooth white hair. "I can't say for a certainty I wouldn't have tried it. But in truth the thought never even occurred to me."

"I'm relieved to hear it."

"Do you believe me?"

"I think so, sir." Malcolm stepped back, prepared to turn to the door. "Which, coming from me, is a fair degree of certainty."

There were two other people Malcolm needed to speak with before he went downstairs to join Andrew. He left his grandfather's suite and crossed the central passage to the bedchamber allotted to Prince Talleyrand. Talleyrand opened the door himself. He was fully dressed, in a frock coat and diamond buckled shoes, his wig powdered and securely in place on his head, though after a brief appearance at breakfast he had retreated upstairs. As befitted a guest in the wake of family tragedy. And yet Talleyrand had been friends with the Duke of Strathdon long before Malcolm was born. He had come to Dunmykel in secret because he and Strathdon had concocted a plan they claimed would allow Malcolm and Mélanie to return to their life in Britain. A plan Malcolm had no intention of risking putting into practice.

All of which suddenly seemed irrelevant in the wake of recent events.

"I assume you're off to look for Gisèle," Talleyrand said.

"With Andrew. And our search will most likely take us to London. Where a week ago on Christmas night I told you I wouldn't risk returning to, despite your kind offer. The irony isn't lost on me."

"The board has shifted."

Malcolm surveyed the prince. He had first met Talleyrand as a boy of five, when the prince sought refuge in England from the Reign of Terror. They had crossed diplomatic swords at the Congress of Vienna and in Paris after Waterloo, though Malcolm had also found Talleyrand an ally who went out of his way to protect Mélanie. "I don't know how long I'll be gone, but I suspect you'll have left for France by the time I return."

"Possibly." Talleyrand cast a glance at the connecting door to the room occupied by his nephew's wife, Dorothée. "I don't wish to leave so long as our presence can give support to your grandfather. I'm quite fond of your sister as well, you know. And I know Dorothée will be concerned about Mélanie."

"You've been a good friend to our family," Malcolm said with truth. He stepped forwards, where the light gave him a better view of Talleyrand's face. One needed all the help one could get to read the prince's expression. "Aunt Frances and Raoul wonder if Gelly may have run because she's trying to learn who her father is."

"And you think Arabella might have told me when she didn't tell her sister or her longest-term lover?"

"She told you about Tatiana."

Talleyrand had helped conceal the birth of Tatiana, Malcolm's illegitimate half-sister, and had watched over her during her childhood in France and later made her his agent. "Actually your grandfather told me about Tatiana," Talleyrand said. "Or rather told me Arabella was with child, at seventeen and unwed, and they needed my assistance. Which of course I was happy to give. There'd have been no such reason for Arabella to confide in me about Gisèle's parentage."

Malcolm held the prince's gaze with his own. "Which wouldn't stop you from having suspicions."

"True enough." Talleyrand's gaze was as shrewd and inscrutable as it was across the negotiating table, yet tinged with warmth. "I counted your mother a friend Malcolm. I flatter myself that she shared things with me that she didn't with many others. And I with her. Perhaps more than I should have done. But she wasn't in the habit of talking about her lovers. And yet—"

Malcolm knew that look in the prince's eyes. Weighing information, weighing how much to say. "What?" he asked. His voice came out sharper than he intended.

Talleyrand glanced down at the buckle on his shoe, sparkling in the light from the fire blazing in the grate. "I was busy with France's concerns at the time your sister would have been conceived. But I did see Arabella once when she was pregnant with Gisèle. Arabella came to France in secret to see Tatiana as she did frequently. She stopped to see me. She wanted to talk about Tatiana. And she had concerns about the Uprising that was brewing in Ireland. She wanted my assurances that I'd help O'Roarke if he needed to flee the country. Which some time later he did indeed need to do."

"And you were indeed of assistance as I hear it."

"Yes, I believe I was. Not for entirely altruistic reasons. I've always found O'Roarke useful. But I've always liked him as well. In any case, that was all in the future when Arabella was with child. We didn't speak much of her pregnancy, but I offered her my wishes for a safe delivery. She said—" Talleyrand stared into the fire, his expression oddly arrested. "She curved her hand round her stomach, much as I've seen Frances and Lady Tarrington do in the past days, much as I've seen many pregnant women do through the years. She said she wasn't unhappy to be having another child. But that she feared the pregnancy might be a mistake that would come back to haunt her."

Malcolm held Talleyrand's keen blue gaze. "Because of the father."

"Presumably."

"Arabella was apparently at pains to keep his identity secret. Unusual pains."

"And that makes you think there may be political ramifications?" Talleyrand asked.

"There's something that made her determined to keep it from Aunt Frances in particular." Malcolm studied the prince. "You must have wondered?"

"Obviously. But as I said I knew few details of her personal life in those months."

Malcolm was aware of the list Raoul had given him tucked inside his coat. His mother's love affairs had been a part of so many investigations he could almost speak of them with equanimity. Almost. "It's no secret Arabella had lovers in her pursuit of the Elsinore League."

Talleyrand twitched a frilled shirt cuff smooth. "The thought of course occurred to me at the time. I confess I even made inquiries of one or two agents in London. Arabella was unusually circumspect in her personal life in the weeks round which your sister must have been conceived."

"Gelly never asked you about the League, did she?"

"No. But that doesn't mean she didn't have suspicions. Your sister is an astute young woman, Malcolm. It runs in the family."

"And I begin to think trying to protect her may have been one of my worst mistakes."

Talleyrand continued to watch Malcolm. "If I knew who Gisèle's father is, or knew anything that I thought would help you find your sister, I'd tell you, my boy."

131

That was quite an admission coming from Talleyrand.
Malcolm almost believed it.

The last person Malcolm had to see was his cousin Aline, who was like a sister to Gisèle. He found her in an upstairs sitting room. Her husband had taken their daughter downstairs to play with the younger children. Allie had never been overly demonstrative, but she crossed right to Malcolm and hugged him tight.

Malcolm's arms closed round his young cousin.

Allie pulled her head back and looked up at him. "I keep thinking I should have seen something. I was so busy with that wretched code on Boxing Day—"

"That code may prove vital." It had revealed that his mother had intercepted information two decades ago that both the Elsinore League and Malcolm's former spymaster, Lord Carfax, were suddenly bent on finding.

"None of us saw anything, Allie," Malcolm said. "Gelly hadn't said anything recently to make you think she was planning anything?"

"No. Well—" Aline frowned. "Yesterday morning we were playing with the children, and she looked at Ian crawling after Claudia and said it was good he'd always have so many people to love him." She looked at Malcolm, in that fearless way she'd always been able to confront hard truths. "Do you think she was planning to leave then?"

"I don't know," Malcolm said honestly. "But I don't see how you could possibly have guessed it if she was. Allie—did Gelly ever seem curious about her father?"

Aline's blue eyes widened. "You think that's why she left?"

"It's one possible reason."

Aline rubbed her arms. "We talked about it off and on growing up. But not as much as you'd think, considering neither of us knew. We hadn't discussed it in years. But only a week ago—no a bit more, it was before Christmas—we were wrapping presents in the old drawing room. And she suddenly asked me if I ever wondered about my father. I said truthfully that I had much more important things to think about these days and it really didn't matter. Gelly got an odd look in her eyes. She said she used to feel that way. But lately she'd been thinking it might matter more than she'd ever have dreamed possible."

MIDWINTER INTRIGUE

Malcolm found Mélanie in the study with Andrew. Andrew was frowning, as though in contemplation, but at Malcolm's entrance he rose and moved to the door. "I'll see if the carriage is ready."

Andrew had always been tactful. This was probably his and Mel's last chance for a private goodbye.

Mélanie got to her feet as well and gestured to a valise beside her chair. "All the essentials."

Malcolm nodded and crossed to her side, but instead of taking the valise, he put his hands on her shoulders. God knows he'd left often enough—too often—during the war, but on missions within Spain. The dangers may have been worse, but his return hadn't been so open-ended. And she hadn't been at nearly as much risk herself. "Promise me—"

"At the least hint of danger I'll leave for Italy."

Malcolm looked down into his wife's face. He remembered saying goodbye to her the first time he'd left after their marriage. The same brilliant sea-green eyes and winged brows and ironic mouth. Yet he knew her so much better now. "Why do I not believe that?"

"Darling." She put her hands on his where they rested on her shoulders. "We have to trust each other to make the right choices."

He took her face between his hands. "The stakes have never been higher, sweetheart. And we've never been a continent apart."

"And if things go well, we won't be." Her throat tightened. "We always find our way back to each other. It's a bit redundant, but be careful yourself, darling."

He kissed her and pulled her into a tight embrace, committing to memory the taste of her mouth, the scent of her skin, the softness of her hair.

Somehow, the longer they were together, the more he was aware how fragile everything between them was.

Mélanie clung to him for a moment, then pressed her lips to his cheek. "I love you, darling. Don't forget that until I'm here to tell you again."

About the Author

Tracy Grant studied British history at Stanford University and received the Firestone Award for Excellence in Research for her honors thesis on shifting conceptions of honor in late-fifteenth-century England. She lives in the San Francisco Bay Area with her young daughter and three cats. In addition to writing, Tracy works for the Merola Opera Program, a

professional training program for opera singers, pianists, and stage directors. Her real life heroine is her daughter Mélanie, who is very cooperative about Mummy's writing time. She is currently at work on her next book chronicling the adventures of Malcolm and Mélanie Suzanne Rannoch. Visit her on the Web at www.tracygrant.org

Author photo: Raphael Coffey Photography